RED DOVE

Listen to the Wind

One Elm Books is an imprint of Red Chair Press LLC
www.redchairpress.com

Publisher's Cataloging-In-Publication Data

Names: Antaki, Sonia. | Bosley, Andrew, illustrator. | Spotted Elk,
Calvin, writer of supplementary textual content.

Title: Red Dove, listen to the wind / by Sonia Antaki ; with illustrations
by Andrew Bosley ; [foreword by Calvin Spotted Elk, Lakota].

Description: Egremont, Massachusetts : One Elm Books, an imprint of Red
Chair Press LLC, [2019] | Includes Lakota terms and phrases. | Interest
age level: 010-014. | Summary: "Abandoned by her white father,
thirteen-year-old Red Dove faces another lean winter with her Lakota
family on the Great Plains. Willful and proud, she is presented with a
difficult choice: leave her people to live in the white world, or stay
and watch them starve. Red Dove begins a journey to find her true place
in the world and discovers that her greatest power comes from within
herself."--Provided by publisher.

Identifiers: ISBN 9781947159129 (hardcover) | ISBN 9781947159136
(paperback) | ISBN 9781947159143 (ebook)

Subjects: LCSH: Indian girls--Juvenile fiction. | Racially mixed youth--
Juvenile fiction. | Identity (Psychology) in youth--Juvenile fiction. |
Lakota Indians--United States--History--19th century--Juvenile fiction.
| CYAC: Indian girls--Fiction. | Identity--Fiction. | Lakota Indians--
United States--History--19th century--Fiction. | LCGFT: Historical
fiction.

Classification: LCC PZ7.1.A61 Re 2019 (print) | LCC PZ7.1.A61 (ebook) |
DDC [Fic]--dc23

LC record available at https://lccn.loc.gov/2018955613

Main body text set in 13/18.5 Adobe Caslon Pro

Text copyright © 2020 by Sonia Antaki

One Elm Books, logo and green leaf colophon are trademarks of
Red Chair Press LLC.

Printed in Canada

0519 1P FNF19

MIX
Paper from
responsible sources
FSC
www.fsc.org   FSC® C016245

RED DOVE

Listen to the Wind

BY SONIA ANTAKI

WITH ILLUSTRATIONS BY ANDREW BOSLEY

This is an original story,
Dedicated to my Goddaughter, Lily Spotted Elk, Lakota—
Descendant of the man who led his people at Wounded Knee

Introduction

I first met Sonia at an event I was hosting for Chief Arvol Looking Horse, (the 19th keeper of the Sacred White Buffalo Calf Pipe). After striking up a friendly conversation, I could see that we were kindred spirits of sorts. Subsequent visits revealed that she was writing a book for young readers about a 13-year old half-Lakota, half-white girl.

Since my own ancestry dates back to include my Great Grandfather, Wiyaka Sakpe (Six Feathers), who rode with Crazy Horse in "The Battle of Little Big Horn", or as our people refer to as "The Battle of the Greasy Grass", it seemed only natural that I would help with a few details to make the story more "authentic", even though it is a work of fiction.

Red Dove, Listen to the Wind is a tale of a mixed-blood girl who struggles to bring her worlds together. It is an entertaining work that shares the Native American experience of a turbulent time in U.S. history with our world today.

As the story unfolds, you feel the angst of an adolescent girl who has a lust for life, but who is riddled with frustration, curiosity and a little rebellion for good measure—something most young people still experience.

I read it non-stop, alternating between scolding this precocious youngster and cheering her tenacious search for a place to belong.

Red Dove, Listen to the Wind is a good read for all ages.

–Linda Sixfeathers, Lakota Sioux

CANADA
Fort Peck
Missouri R.
Fort Union
Fort Berthold
Fort Stevenson
Fort Clarke
MONTANA TERRITORY
Bismarck
Standing Rock Agency
Red R. of the North
Fort Abercrombie
Yellowstone R.
DAKOTA TERRITORY
CROW COUNTRY
Great Sioux Agency
Fort Sully
ARAKARA COUNTRY
THE BLACK HILLS
Cheyenne R.
Cheyenne Agency
Deadwood
LAKOTA COUNTRY
Jerusha's cabin
The school
Fort Randall
Pine Ridge Agency
Red Dove's village
Wounded Knee
Rosebud Agency
Fort Robinson
WYOMING TERRITORY
NEBRASKA
North Platte R.
Fort Laramie
Fort Gratton
Fort Hartsuff
PAWNEE COUNTRY
Fort Halleck
Cheyenne
South Platte R.
Fort Mc Pherson
Fort Kearny
CHEYENNE COUNTRY
COLORADO
Fort Hays
Fort Wallace
KANSAS
Fort Granada
UNORGANIZED TERRITORY
NEW MEXICO TERRITORY

Foreword

When Sonia Antaki asked me to consult for *Red Dove, Listen to the Wind*, I agreed, because I knew how important it was to bring this story of traveling between worlds, told through the eyes of a thirteen-year-old girl, to an audience of new readers.

I am Lakota, and my daughter Lily and I are descended from the man who led our people at Wounded Knee. The history books call him Chief Big Foot—Si Tanka—but his true name was Spotted Elk—Unpan Gleska—the name that my daughter and I carry now.

Like many Lakota growing up on South Dakota's Pine Ridge Reservation in the 1970s, my childhood was marked by poverty and loss. I know what it is to attend a school like the one described in the story. I also know what it is to live with the legacy of Wounded Knee.

Red Dove, Listen to the Wind is a work of fiction, but it tells a tale that resonates still, in the hopes that some young reader, boy or girl, will grow up to help right the wrongs that have been visited on our people for far, far too long.

–Calvin Spotted Elk, Lakota

Kantasa Wi

The Moon-of-Ripe-Plums

Dakota Territory—Late Summer, 1890

"**G**irls don't hunt," Red Dove's brother said. "So go away!"

Red Dove pretended not to hear. She pointed to the flock of wild turkeys squawking and squabbling in the meadow below. "We'll go hungry if you miss again, Walks Alone, so let me try." She pulled her brother's ash wood bow out of his hand.

He jerked it back. "I'm not letting you use my arrows," he said, glaring.

"I don't need yours. I have my own. Wait here." Red Dove darted towards the old cottonwood tree. Scrambling up to the knothole, she pulled out her secret treasure: a quiver of arrows.

She raced back but her brother was nowhere in sight. "I told you to wait!" she cried.

Branches clawed her face and tore at the fringe of her deerskin robe as she struggled through the dense chokecherry bushes.

She felt a tap on her shoulder and spun around. Walks Alone put a finger to his lips and pointed to a flock of birds. "Over there. You've frightened them and now they're too far away," he said softly.

Red Dove followed the flight of the big, ungainly birds. She glanced back at their village, nestled in the safety of the Black Hills. It was summer's end; the month called the Moon-of-Ripe-Plums, and cold would be coming soon. Smoke from the cooking fires mingled with the sweet smell of *papa*, the dried venison that would see them through the winter.

Red Dove and her brother followed the birds until finally, in the patch of trees at the edge of the meadow, they came upon the flock. "There," she whispered.

Walks Alone pointed at the biggest tom in the center, strutting and fanning its tail. He raised his bow, pulled the string and shot.

The hens set up a shriek and rose, flapping, into the air.

"You missed! Why didn't you let me do it?"

Walks Alone threw down his bow and Red Dove lunged to pick it up. Before he could stop her, she fitted an arrow, pulled back and let fly.

It found its mark and the turkey plummeted to earth.

"What did you just do?" Her brother's eyes were round with disbelief.

Pride and wonder mingled in Red Dove's chest. What *did* I just do?

She raced over and stared at the creature before her,

motionless except for the breeze that ruffled its feathers. Then she looked at the bow in her hand and felt a surge of pleasure.

"I've been practicing. With your bow—"

"You took my bow? You're not supposed to hunt. It's not our way."

"Don't tell Mother. She's always so angry with me," Red Dove said, picturing her mother's face when told her rebellious daughter had broken yet another rule.

"Only if you tell me where you got those arrows." Walks Alone pointed to the buckskin quiver. "They look special, like Grandfather's—"

"*I* made them."

"*You* made them? Did he show you how?"

Red Dove felt her brother's envy. "I just watched him while he was working. Nobody saw me. Mother was too busy and you were always so sick." She flinched when she saw his angry face. "Well, you *were!*"

"Be careful what you say to people, Gray Eyes—"

"Don't call me Gray Eyes. I can't help it if my father was white."

Her brother shrugged. "You're right; it's not your fault. But you should know better. You've lived thirteen winters. You're old enough now to respect our ways." He reached down and plucked the longest tail feather from the dead tom. "Here." He pushed it into Red Dove's tightly wound braid. "For your coming-of-age ceremony."

"Thank you, Brother—"

"Don't thank me. Thank the animal."

"*Wopila,*" she said, and bowed her head to thank the creature that had given its life.

>> *Wasichu* <<

Red Dove and her brother carried their kill through the forest to the clearing. Walks Alone moved steadily ahead, the bird slung over his shoulder. Red Dove followed until they came to the glistening stream their mother loved.

"We have a surprise!" Red Dove called when she saw their mother sitting on a lichen-covered stone.

Falling Bird smiled at her handsome son. "What have you got there?"

Resentment curled inside Red Dove. *Why does she always look at him—and not at me?*

Walks Alone threw the bird on the ground and grinned. "A turkey," he said.

"But I'm the one who brought it down," Red Dove blurted.

The look of shock on her mother's face frightened Red Dove. "What? Have I raised you so badly that you do not know your place?" said Falling Bird. "Girls don't hunt—unless they have to."

Red Dove bowed her head, filled with sudden shame.

"These things are taught so we can live in balance."

"Yes, Mother," Red Dove said. *Why is it I can't ever seem to do things right? Is it because I'm half white?*

"Listen," her brother said and cocked his head. They all heard it then: the clatter of cart wheels and the beat of horses' hooves. Soon, they saw the source of the sound.

Wasichu! Red Dove thought. *White people... sometimes they bring food.*

She scrambled towards them, but her mother pulled her back. "Wait here."

But Red Dove wasn't afraid and her curiosity was stronger

than Falling Bird's grasp. She broke away to follow the wagon as it rolled into their village.

A crowd gathered around the two whites who were sitting in the carriage. The few men who remained in the village stood silently by, while anxious mothers held tight to their children.

Red Dove's grandfather crossed the ground towards them. Gray Eagle was thin-boned and short of stature, but his frail body held a power his people knew well. He lifted his head and stared out of age-clouded eyes.

Red Dove's mother wagged a finger and warned her to stay back, but Red Dove edged closer.

A gaunt, leather-faced man in dirty denim and sweat-stained buckskin climbed off the wagon, his battered gray hat pulled low over red-rimmed eyes. I've seen him before, Red Dove thought. He's the one they call Old Tom, the white man who speaks our language. He's *Iyeska*... a traveler between our worlds.

Old Tom said something to the plump, pink-faced woman in the carriage. Her pale blue eyes behind silvery glasses were soft and frightened, and a drop of sweat rolled from under her lacy black headdress. She tugged at a faded gray shawl that kept slipping off her shoulders over the shiny purple dress that clung to her curves.

White women dress so strangely, thought Red Dove. Women in our village would be ashamed to wear tight clothes like that. And her hair is a funny color, almost orange... .

The woman squinted at Old Tom, but did not climb down.

Red Dove's grandfather raised his hand in greeting.

The woman said something in a language that Red Dove recognized as English, from what she had learned from her mother and brother, who had lived with the whites.

When the woman had finished, Old Tom began to translate so they all could understand. "It has been decided," he said, "that the Lakota people should learn to live like white men—"

Red Dove's mother gasped.

Would that be terrible? Red Dove wondered.

"There isn't enough food for you here," Old Tom continued. "Summer is over and winter will soon come." He looked back at the woman, took off his grimy hat and wiped his brow. He ran his fingers through the wisps of hair still clinging to his head and mumbled something. The woman nodded and said something more.

Kicking up a clod of dirt, Old Tom put his hat back on. "The U.S. government will give you food if you send your children to the school and live on the reservation like the rest of your people have done... ." He seemed startled by the words the woman was making him say.

Red Dove watched her mother's face. Her mouth was set in a firm line, but tears were pooling in her eyes.

When Old Tom had finished, Gray Eagle raised his head and stared at the *Wasichu* woman. "We are hungry. Our young men are gone and there are no more buffalo. You have killed them all." He stared into the distance. "We have heard about your schools... and what happens there. You want us to live on the reservation and trade our children for food?" He paused and lowered his head. "No."

He nodded at Old Tom, who began translating to the woman. She frowned and said something back.

"This is different," Old Tom said, echoing her words in Lakota. "The school we are talking about was started by the priests, the ones your leader Red Cloud invited—"

"Red Cloud is *not* our leader. And *we* did not invite them."

"If you do not let them go," Old Tom went on, not daring to meet the old man's eyes, "the soldiers will come. And take them. By force."

A trickle of fear crept down Red Dove's spine.

Gray Eagle stared at the woman. She stared back. Neither spoke. Then he raised his hand to signal he was finished and moved closer to the fire. When the smoke had cleared, Grandfather was gone.

The white woman looked frantically around. She shrieked something to Old Tom, but he just shrugged and climbed calmly onto the wagon. Then he flicked the reins and the horses jerked away, jostling the woman's floppy headdress loose.

She grabbed it just in time as her small, light-colored eyes fell on Red Dove. Now, they were no longer afraid. Now they looked cold, hard, determined. "I'll be back," they seemed to say.

>> Even If We All Go Hungry <<

Smoke from the council tent rose in a curl and drifted into the sky as the village waited to hear the fate of their children. At last, Gray Eagle came out. He strode past the fire circle and disappeared inside his own dwelling.

"Stay here," Red Dove's mother hissed, but Red Dove pulled away. Something strange was happening and the only one who could explain it was the *wicasa wakan*, the medicine man, Gray Eagle himself. She pulled up the flap and entered the tent.

"I'm sorry, Grandfather," Red Dove said, "but I have to know. Will the white people really make me leave? I want to stay here."

The furrows on his face deepened. "If things were like they were in the past, you would go to the women for answers. Your aunties would be guiding you—"

"But everything is different now, you say. My aunties are so busy finding food they don't have time for me." She paused and smiled up at him. "That's why I'm asking you."

"*Hau, Takoja,*" he said, patting her head and answering yes to his favorite grandchild. Then he sighed. "I know you want to stay here with me, but there may be nothing for you—"

"There is. I want you to teach me to be a healer. Like you."

"It takes a lifetime to be a healer—"

"I can wait."

The old man raised an eyebrow and laughed. "You've never waited for anything in your life." Then he softened his gaze. "Tell me why you want that," he said. "Is it because you want to help others?"

Red Dove nodded. "And I want people to listen to me, and what I have to say… like they do to you."

"Ahhh. Then you must learn to listen—to *them*—"

"I do."

"You do not." Gray Eagle pressed his lips together. "You ask many questions, little Gray Eyes, but when the answers come you do not hear them—"

"Don't call me that!"

"What, Gray Eyes? But your eyes *are* gray. Gray like the dawn—"

"I can't help being different, Grandfather; you know that!" Red Dove looked at the ashy fire, as if to take courage from the smoke rising from it. "Is that why no one listens to me? Because I am half... *Wasichu*?"

The old man smiled and placed his hand gently on top of her head. "You are different, but not just because your father was white." He removed his hand and turned away. "And some day you will see that as a gift," he said quietly. "You will be special—"

"Special? How?"

"You will be *Iyeska*—"

"An interpreter, like Old Tom? I want to be like you."

"I am *Iyeska*, as you will be also. And more. You will have the gift of understanding, of what is behind the words that people speak. You will travel between worlds—"

"What worlds, Grandfather? The world of the whites, the *Wasichu*?"

"Worlds you cannot yet imagine," he whispered. "You will travel between them, explain them to others and bring them together."

Red Dove wanted to shout at him. Nothing was making any sense. She stared at his hunched figure and dared to ask the question that had plagued her since the white people came. "So, will you send me away?"

Gray Eagle turned. "Only if you want to go, Granddaughter." He placed his hand on her shoulder and she felt its reassuring weight. "We will not make you. Even if it means we go hungry." He tilted her face up towards his. "Remember, we are the last of a free people."

Red Dove breathed a sigh and felt the knot inside her

begin to loosen. She nodded.

Gray Eagle smiled and pointed at the flap of the tepee. "Now go. And be the child you still are—"

"I'm not a child, Grandfather—you know that. I'm almost a woman. I'll have my coming-of-age soon—"

"Perhaps."

"*Perhaps?* Why do you say that?"

The old man didn't answer.

The relief that Red Dove had felt disappeared.

"Now go and tell Falling Bird that her children will not leave," Gray Eagle murmured, "even if we all go hungry."

"But Grandfather—" Red Dove began, knowing that he was not going to answer. He sat in his customary pose, legs crossed, eyes closed, listening to something—just not to her.

So Red Dove did as she was told. She pulled up the flap and crawled outside into the late-summer day.

There's just so much I don't understand.

>> All You Need to Know <<

Red Dove returned to her tepee and found Falling Bird squatting inside with her back to the opening. Her shoulders were shaking.

"Mother?"

There was no answer.

"Mother?" Red Dove inched closer.

Her mother turned to look at her, eyes glistening with tears. Strands of silver ran through her hair—more than Red Dove remembered.

When did she get so old? Red Dove wondered. But what I have to say will cheer her up. "Grandfather says we won't have to go to the school," she said.

"*Washte*. Good," Falling Bird said, as a smile lifted the corners of her mouth.

"But we will be hungry—"

"*Han*. Yes, we will. But we can trade our beadwork for food. And Walks Alone can hunt."

Red Dove longed to tell Falling Bird that she was the real hunter in the family—but didn't. She'll only be mad at me again.

"Maybe the person who used to leave food outside our lodge will come back," Falling Bird said.

"Do you know who it was?"

Her mother shook her head.

"Do you think it was my father?"

"*Hiya*, no!" Falling Bird said. "Do not speak of him!"

"But why? You've never told me what happened." Red Dove tried to sound calm. "You said we lived with him when I was little, and then he left. Did you do something… ," Red Dove knew she should stop, but couldn't. She asked the question she had wanted so long to ask. "To make him go away?"

Her mother didn't look at her. Instead, she rose slowly, pulled up the flap and left the tent.

Red Dove poked her head through the opening. "Mother?" she called.

"Follow me."

So Red Dove did, past the fire circle and cluster of tepees, across the grassy meadow, and towards the patch of cottonwood trees that fringed the little stream.

My mother's quiet place, Red Dove thought, as fear sparked through her. Why is she bringing me here?

"Sit," Falling Bird ordered. "It is time you learned the truth. About your father." Her shoulders slumped, light drained from her eyes, and the lines in her face were etched deep by the brightness of morning. "He left because he didn't care. He betrayed us. And left us to starve—"

"Then why were you with him, if he was so terrible?"

"Ah," her mother sighed. "How can I explain it? He was kind at first. I thought he loved me... us—"

"Did *you* love him?"

"*Han.* But something happened. He changed. He was *Wasichu*, so he didn't keep his promise—"

"Why not?"

"He deserted us." Falling Bird searched her daughter's face. "And I don't want him to hurt us anymore. Do you understand that?"

Red Dove saw the pain in her mother's eyes. It was too much.

"You don't remember anything of him, do you?"

Do I? Maybe. "But why did he change?" she dared to ask.

"White people change. We do not."

But I'm half white, so what does that mean for me?

Falling Bird slapped her knee and rose abruptly. "So now I've told you all you need to know."

The bright prairie morning was thick with the scent of sweet grass and sage as Red Dove watched her mother walk away. She shook her head to clear it, filled as it was with memories just out of reach. "Wait," she called softly, sensing Falling Bird was already too far away to hear. "You haven't really told me anything!"

>> We're Going to the Fort <<

"Get up, daughter."

Red Dove opened her eyes. The first light of dawn was visible below the flap of the tent, but sleep was sweet and she didn't want to wake.

Her mother pulled a worn woolen blanket around her shoulders. "We're going to the fort today to trade with the *Wasichu*."

All summer long they had beaded moccasins and pouches to exchange for the flour, sugar, coffee, and oil they needed, and with a hard winter approaching, it was more important than ever that they make a good trade.

The fort was a dangerous place, everyone said, filled with treacherous *Wasichu*, but Red Dove looked forward to the sights.

She braided her hair carefully, making sure that the two long plaits fell neatly behind her ears. She pulled her bead necklace over her head and slung the roomy *parfleche* bag across her chest. Her robe was missing a few of the precious quills that decorated the bodice and her leggings and moccasins were worn thin in patches. In spite of that, she was proud to wear her deerskin. She tugged her blanket around her shoulders. "I'm ready," she called.

"I want to give you something first." In Falling Bird's hand was a beaded amulet in the shape of a turtle. "This is your *opahte*. It holds the cord that connected me to you when you were born. I've been keeping it for you."

Red Dove picked up the little bag by its leather thong and studied the bright blue and yellow beadwork. "It's beautiful," she whispered.

"It's been watching over you all these years. I was going to give it to you at your coming-of-age ceremony." Her mother reached for the little object. "So here, let me." Stepping behind Red Dove, she pushed aside her daughter's thick black braids and circled her slender neck with the thong. Then she tied it securely in back. "Don't let anything happen to it," she whispered, as she turned Red Dove gently and smiled into her face. "Now go and tell your brother that we are leaving. *Wana*. Now."

"Is he coming with us?"

Falling Bird shook her head.

"But why? We need him to carry, don't we?"

"Carrying is woman's work. And he's still too weak. "

"Not any more, he isn't," Red Dove began.

"Show respect, daughter. *Hoka*. Let's go."

I *do*, thought Red Dove, as the tenderness she felt dissolved in the thin morning air. I just wish other people would show some respect for me.

>> We Do Not Eat the Fruit <<

Scents of wood smoke, sweetgrass and sage filled the crisp morning air as Red Dove and Falling Bird set off down the hill and onto the grassy plain. They carried roomy *parfleche* bags, one stuffed with their precious beadwork, the other empty, waiting to be filled at the fort.

"Why is this women's work?" Red Dove asked.

"What?" Her mother swatted at a bee buzzing around her.

"The bags will be heavy when they're full. Shouldn't Walks Alone help us?"

"Men don't carry. And he's still sick."

He's been sick ever since he came back from the white man's school, Red Dove thought. "I wish we had a pony to ride," she muttered instead.

"I do too, but we don't, so stop talking about it."

"What will they give us in trade?"

Her mother stopped and swung the stiff *parfleche* bags from one shoulder to the other. "I told you. Flour, sugar, lard maybe," she said with a sigh.

"To make fry bread? I'll help you cook it."

"You'd better, since you like eating it so much," Falling Bird said with a faint smile.

Red Dove, pleased to see her mother happy, felt her spirits lighten. She watched the sun climb overhead as they started across the grassy meadow. Distant bluffs, pink and purple in the morning light, began to fade and the early chill blended into the heat of noon.

Now she was thirsty. "Water," she whispered, through parching lips.

Falling Bird stopped and thrust the bulging skin towards her. "Here," she said.

Red Dove took a gulp.

"Slow down. Leave some for the way back. There won't be any in the *Wasichu* town—"

"*Wasichu* don't have water?"

"Of course they do." Her mother's face turned serious. "Just not for us."

"We would share, wouldn't we?"

"Yes," said Falling Bird. "But they don't think and feel as we do."

"Why not?"

15

Falling Bird stopped dead. "Would you please stop asking me so many questions?"

Disappointed, Red Dove went silent.

By now her stomach hurt, a reminder that she hadn't eaten since the sun was high the day before. There, up ahead, was a low bush covered with shiny purple fruit.

Plums. Her mouth watered as she imagined how good one would taste. "Look."

Her mother's anger was swift. "That is the Dead Man's Plum Bush—"

"The one Grandfather talks about in his stories?"

"The same. You know we do not eat the fruit," said Falling Bird.

Red Dove stared at the ripe, juicy plums left rotting on the ground, insects swarming above them. "Those bees aren't afraid—"

"Enough." Her mother wheeled around and glared at her.

"But they *aren't* afraid," insisted Red Dove, as she watched the creatures feasting on the sticky pulp, "so why should I be?"

She looked at her mother shuffling ahead, too far away to hear. She listened to the sounds all around: the scrape of moccasins against the sandy soil, the growl in her belly that rumbled and churned, and the drone of bees as they devoured the delicious fruit that she was forbidden to touch.

≫ Soldiers ≪

Red Dove followed her mother along the well-worn path, dawdling until a row of flat-roofed log buildings came into view.

Everything here is sharp and angular, she observed, not like the rounded, comfortable dwellings in our village.

Her heart beat faster and she closed the gap. "Is that it?"

"*Han.* That's where the soldiers live. You know what happened there, don't you?"

Red Dove remembered what her grandfather had told them. This was where the soldiers had imprisoned Dull Knife and his people before sending them back to the reservation, where they would sicken and die of disease and starvation and where the soldiers shot them down when they tried to escape—men, women, and children alike.

Red Dove felt a sudden chill. It was just past midday, but the sun had vanished behind a cloud and in its place was thick, dark shadow. The light had changed so swiftly that for a moment it was hard to see.

Their ghosts must still be here. Do the soldiers know that?

She didn't have long to think about it. She turned a corner and saw a mass of people, crowded into the center of a square, more than she had ever seen in her life.

They look like women from my village... but different somehow.

Instead of deerskin, they wore frayed calico with blankets pulled over their shoulders. Their faces were dull and vacant, their bodies hunched. Then she saw a girl, about her age, whose eyes were drained of life.

"What's wrong with her, Mother?"

"Come," ordered Falling Bird, pulling her towards the low, straight-lined buildings on the other side of the square.

"But why are they here?"

"Getting food from the *Wasichu*—"

17

"Like we are?"

"No." Her mother stopped abruptly. "*We* have things the *Wasichu* want that we can trade," she said. "*They* are here to beg. We do not. No more questions," she warned.

They reached the far end of the courtyard and saw a cluster of blue-coated soldiers playing cards, laughing, shouting, and banging metal cups. Odd, screechy music came from inside the bunkhouse.

Red Dove felt her mother's hand tighten around her own.

She's afraid, she thought. Then she saw why.

"Hey!" a soldier with greasy yellow hair and a black eye-patch called. "Whatcha got? Lemme see."

Red Dove understood the few words of English, but it was his scowl that told her he wasn't friendly. She watched him walk towards them and felt the blood freeze in her veins.

Falling Bird kept walking.

"Lemme see whatcha got, I said."

"*Inahnio*," her mother said, urging her to hurry. They rushed past the soldier's one glaring eye and up onto the wood-plank sidewalk.

"Indians" muttered the man.

A tawny-faced boy in a blue uniform, his arms around a scruffy yellow dog, knelt in the dirt, watching them.

"Sic 'em, Spirit," the man yelled.

The boy wrapped his arms tighter around the squirming animal. "No!" he shouted as the dog wriggled free.

Falling Bird looked wildly around, searching for a place to hide. She pulled Red Dove behind a pillar.

But the mongrel wasn't after them. Leaping and snarling, it went for the one-eyed man.

18

"Whaaa?!" shouted the man as the dog locked its jaw around his leg. He pulled out his gun.

"Don't, Jake!" The boy raced over and hauled the animal away.

A soldier with snow-white hair threw down his cards and limped over. "Give me the gun," he said.

Jake's fingers twitched on the trigger as he glared at the white-haired man.

"Give it to me, Private."

Jake looked at the man, then lowered his eyes. "Yessir, Cap'n," he said.

The captain took the gun, emptied the chamber and put the bullets in his pocket. "Just in case," he said. He hobbled back to the table and picked up his cards.

Red Dove watched the one-eyed man slink away. Then she noticed her mother. Her eyes were fixed on the white-haired soldier. "Do you know him?" Red Dove asked.

Her mother didn't answer. Instead, she turned away and pulled her blanket over her head.

She doesn't want him to see her... why? Red Dove studied the man. Middle-aged and paunchy, he wore a uniform covered with gold-colored metal. He must be someone important.

When he dropped back into his chair, raised a flask to his lips, and reached for his cards again, she noticed his arm was bent at an odd angle.

Like it had been broken—and healed wrong.

Then she looked at the boy, still holding his dog, his face buried in its scruffy fur.

She smiled at him, but crouched over the animal, he didn't see. She was about to say something when the one-eyed man turned and walked back to the boy.

"*Hiya*," she cried. "No."

Too late. Jake took aim and gave the animal a hard, swift kick.

The dog howled in pain.

"For the love of Christ," shouted the captain.

"I hate mutts," snarled Jake. He turned his one good eye on Red Dove. "Indians too."

Red Dove raced up behind her mother onto the rough plank sidewalk, as far away from the one-eyed man as she could possibly get.

>> You Dropped Something <<

They came to a rickety screen door that squawked as it opened. Behind it was a little, round-faced white woman in a shiny purple dress.

She's the one who came to our village.

The woman narrowed her eyes at them and raised her chin as she tried to shove through, but her enormous skirt caught between the door and the frame until finally, after tugging and twisting, she worked her way free.

"*Excuse me*," she sniffed, as the door slammed behind her.

Red Dove watched her go. "That's the woman—"

"I know. Hurry," Falling Bird said, pushing the door open again.

Red Dove looked in at the shelves piled high with bags and boxes and metal things, more than she had ever seen in one place.

"Hello," her mother called to the man standing behind a

wooden counter.

"Whatcha want?" he said.

"Mista Reed?"

"Not here. Go away."

"We trade... *Washte*... ."

"*Washte*? Don't speak Indian."

"*Washte* mean... good," Falling Bird tried. "Mista Reed say—"

"Reed ain't here, I tell you. Now go away," snarled the man.

Her mother reached into her *parfleche* and pulled out a pouch. "Good... *washte*," she said, and tried to lay it on the counter. "You like." But her voice was shaking.

The man raised his fist and lunged, sending everything flying. He grabbed a pouch and threw it at them. "Get out, I said!" Blue and yellow crystals skittered around the room.

Red Dove snatched the *parfleche*, grabbed as much as she could, and she and her mother raced out the door. Eyes to the ground, they ran across the courtyard, past the card-playing soldiers, the strange white-haired man, and the line of ragged women.

When at last they reached the far end, they stopped to catch their breath. Red Dove felt something behind her. The boy... .

"Is your dog all right?" she called in her own language.

"Huh?"

Red Dove pointed to the animal.

The boy nodded.

"*Washte*... good," said Red Dove.

The boy raised his hand. "You dropped something." He

21

pointed back to the courtyard.

The sun was high overhead, the ground without shadow. Red Dove lifted a hand to shield her eyes and squinted.

"Whatcha doin', Rick?" called Jake. "You turnin' into some kinda Indian-lover?"

"Nah," said the boy. "I'm not... Watch this." She saw him, silhouetted against the glare, his arm raised. Something hit her ankle and the pain knocked her speechless.

Stunned, she looked at the boy. She saw the rock on the ground at her feet, the blood oozing from her leg.

"That'll teach 'em, Rick," yelled Jake.

She heard Rick laugh. "Why?" she asked silently.

A cloud swallowed the sun and the light changed, exposing things that weren't visible before. Rick's amber-colored eyes caught Red Dove's. I'm sorry, he seemed to say.

Are you? Red Dove wanted to ask.

"Come. Now," her mother said, frantically pulling her away.

When at last they were safe outside the fort, Falling Bird pointed to the trickle of red seeping from her daughter's leg. "Here," she whispered and picked up a small gray piece of fluff lying on the ground at their feet. She dabbed until the bleeding had stopped and handed the pink-tinged feather to Red Dove. "It's from a dove, your namesake. A good omen, I think, after all that has happened today."

>> The Dead Man's Plum Bush <<

Afternoon shadows lengthened as Red Dove limped slowly along, feeling her ankle throb and the pain in her belly get worse.

"How are you?" her mother said.

"All right," Red Dove lied.

Falling Bird held out the water skin. "Drink. There's enough for the trip back if we're careful."

Red Dove sipped slowly, leaving a few precious drops, and handed it back.

A breeze riffled the grasses that lined the hill, and the sun sank low in the sky as they climbed. The cool air was a relief, but the now-familiar ache of hunger began to claw and there would be nothing to eat that night. "Maybe we should have asked for help from the soldiers, since we didn't get anything from the shopkeeper—"

"We will not beg," her mother hissed. Then her face softened. "I know you're hungry, daughter—we all are. But we cannot listen to the white man's promises. We will find another way to fill our stomachs."

They reached the top of the hill, where Red Dove saw the bush, thick with plums that were ripe to bursting and begging to be picked. "They look delicious," she murmured as she stumbled along, lost in thought.

So much had gone wrong that day; so much that her mother had predicted hadn't happened. Falling Bird had been wrong a lot—wrong about going to town, wrong about white people, wrong about finding food.

One plum couldn't hurt, could it? Fruit that had fallen would only rot and go to waste... .

She slowed her walk and waited until her mother was well ahead and bent down, pretending to rub her burning ankle. Then she reached over and closed her fingers around a plum lying near her foot. Waving off the stinging bees, she picked it up, slipped it between her lips and felt the luscious sweetness explode in her mouth. She sucked on the scratchy little pit until all the meat was gone.

Just one more, she thought, craving the taste of another plum as hunger overcame her.

Suddenly, a *hissssss* and she saw, in the shadows, a coiled shape: bead-black eyes, flitting tongue, and yellow fangs, poised to strike. Terror seized her and she ran, limping and stumbling up the path to her mother.

"What's wrong?"

"Nothing," Red Dove said, wiping her chin with the little plum seed still nestled on her tongue.

Her mother sighed and resumed her walk; when she wasn't looking, Red Dove spat the seed into her hand and tried to throw it in the grass. But her palm was sticky with juice and when she looked down she saw it was stained a deep purple, and the seed was stuck.

She reached out, grabbed a fistful of grass and rubbed and rubbed until the seed fell off. She next scooped up a handful of sandy soil, wiped her palms together, and watched the dust swirl up until her fingers were dry.

Mother will never know, she thought with relief as she waded through the whispering grass.

>> A Purple Stain <<

Fires were lit for the evening meal when Red Dove and her mother got back to the village. Red Dove watched Falling Bird feed the flames with twigs and shreds of wood. "What are you cooking tonight?" she asked.

"Find me something to cook and I will," her mother snapped. Then her voice softened. "The fire is for the night,

Daughter, because it's cold. Go fetch water and we'll drink it with the last of the venison *papa*. That's all we'll have to eat tonight."

Red Dove crawled out of the tepee. The moon was rising full and reflected off the surface of the stream, lighting the world around. She filled the empty water skin and cupped her hand to drink—and saw... .

The stain—it's still there on my palm!

She thrust her hand into the water and scrubbed hard until she was sure it was gone. Looking around to make sure no one had noticed, she picked up the water skin and walked slowly back to the tepee, listening to the voices of her family coming from within.

I worry too much, she thought. Cheered by the promise of light and warmth, she pulled up the flap and crept inside.

Her mother was waiting for her, holding out a small piece of *papa*. "The last of it."

"Shouldn't we save it then?" Red Dove whispered.

"It will make it easier to sleep. Do as I say and eat."

Red Dove reached for the tiny scrap of meat and bit down. She could have devoured it in one swallow, but instead, she broke off a tiny morsel, crept back, lifted the tent flap and tossed the crumb to the hungry ghosts waiting outside.

She caught the look of approval on her mother's face.

We both know it will be licked up by ravenous animals, but after all that's happened today, I don't want to break any more traditions.

Red Dove followed her mother to her grandfather's tepee. She settled herself on the worn buffalo skin and watched him prepare to tell his nightly story.

Falling Bird leaned back against the pile of folded blankets and reached for her daughter's hand. "Things will be all right now," she started to say and then broke off abruptly. She dropped Red Dove's hand as if it burned. "How could you?" she hissed, and pushed her away.

Red Dove looked down and all her dread returned. The purple stain was back.

"Get out," her mother said.

All eyes were on Red Dove as she slowly crawled outside. Alone now, she stared at the moonlit world. The small stream glistened and the trees still rustled in the wind. But somehow everything had changed.

She strained to hear the murmurs coming from the lodge. The sounds no longer cheered her. Now they were scattered, abrupt and anxious, and they frightened her.

What are they saying? Is she telling them what I did?

Once all was quiet, she crouched low and stepped back inside. No one looked at her as she found another place on the women's side of the tent. Gray Eagle stared at the fire as he began his tale.

"The Dead Man's Plum Bush," he announced.

Does he know? Does everyone?

Red Dove's face burned with shame. Desperately, she searched the faces around her. She wanted someone, *anyone*, to tell her that after such a disastrous day, everything would be all right—but no one did.

"We do not touch its fruit," Gray Eagle began, "for its roots are wrapped around the body of a fallen warrior."

I know that, Red Dove thought, bowing her head.

She watched the faces around to see their reaction. The adults were impassive, but her little cousins' eyes were bright, fixed upon the old storyteller as they snuggled in their blankets. Firelight flickered off the walls of the tepee, casting shadows against the light.

"And we would be eating the fruit of his misfortune. Do you understand?" said Gray Eagle, leaning forward. "Our people do not speak of the dead, but I speak of *him* today because this lesson is important for you."

He looked at Red Dove.

"From the seed a bush sprang up, a bush that bears its fruit all year round, in rainless summers and sunless winters, protected by a swarm of bees and a single hissing snake."

His eyes bored into her.

"We do not touch the fruit of loss, for *no one* is beyond the reach of fortune and *everyone* is to be treated with compassion and respect. That is the right way—it is our way—and if we turn from our ways, the circle will be broken, and misfortune will follow."

Red Dove touched her throat and reached for the comfort of the turtle *opahte*.

It wasn't there.

She felt her chest, her waist, her throat in a desperate effort to find it, but the precious gift was gone.

No! she wanted to scream, and lay awake, eyes staring, ears straining, until at last, close to dawn, she heard a sound.

"*Hoo hoo*," it cried.

An owl? Messenger of death?

"*Hoo hoo… hoo hoo hoo.*"

A five-tone trill, she thought, breathing with relief. A

dove, my namesake.

And finally fell asleep.

>> The Apple <<

Sunlight streamed through the top of the tepee as Red Dove woke. Without stopping to smooth her hair or straighten her clothes, she scrambled out.

The smoke from the evening fires mingled with the morning mist. She pulled her blanket close, retraced her steps to the river and followed the path, searching for the turtle amulet.

Her mother was in the clearing, sitting on a log, bent over her beadwork.

Should I tell her I've lost it? She's so angry about the plum. But Red Dove could bear it no longer. She *had* to confess.

"There's something I have to tell you," she blurted, rushing up to her mother.

Falling Bird cut her off. "You disappoint me so much." Her voice was barely above a whisper. "You do not listen. Maybe you can't help it," she went on more gently, "because your father was white."

Her words landed like a blow. Red Dove opened her mouth, but nothing came out.

"You do not respect our ways. You disturbed the dead man's spirit. You have brought us harm."

Moments passed.

"I'm sorry," Red Dove said at last. "What will happen?"

"We do not yet know." Her mother lowered her head. "But it won't be good."

Fear clutched at Red Dove. Could it be that for once

Falling Bird was right?

Then she heard a violent clatter from beyond the trees. She saw Old Tom, perched in his wagon, urging his horses up the hill and making straight for the center of their camp.

Beside him, the white woman called "Hellooo!" as they rolled past and came to a stop near Gray Eagle's tent. She picked up her skirts and climbed carefully down. Then she reached into her dusty black satchel and pulled out a rectangular object with two crossed lines on its cover. "Bible," she said.

She thrust her hand in again and brought out something else, red, round and shiny. Holding it up, she looked straight at Red Dove. "Food. Eat." She put her fingers to her mouth and then her belly.

You don't have to act it out. I know what food is.

The woman launched into louder speech, too rapid for Red Dove to understand. Then she nodded at Old Tom, who began to translate with a question on his face, as if the words were hard for him to say.

The woman wrinkled her forehead and narrowed her eyes. "Let me," she said, brushing him aside. "This is an apple. Ap... ple."

"She wants you to try it," said Old Tom, translating into Lakota. "And *if* you like it, there will be plenty more. For you and your family as well."

It looks good, Red Dove thought, as she listened to yet another growl from her empty belly.

Gray Eagle came out of his lodge, but his expression told her nothing.

"Should I?" she asked her mother.

"No."

"But if I do what the *Wasichu* want, they *might* give us food. I can make up for what I did." She stepped forward and held out her hand.

Her mother snatched at her arm, but Red Dove shrugged her off.

She took the fruit.

And bit.

Washte, good, she thought as her teeth pierced the skin and the warm juice rolled down. It tastes wonderful.

She bit again and a shred of peel cut into the flesh of her gum. Blood and sweetness blended together, and she stared at the unfamiliar fruit. There, against the creamy whiteness of the pulp was a single speck of red.

The woman smiled. She looked at Walks Alone. "This is for you," she said, and held out another piece of fruit.

Gray Eagle knocked it from her hand. "*Hiya!*"

A torrent burst from the white woman's mouth, angry and unintelligible.

Old Tom pulled off his hat, and stared at the ground. "We're trying to do what's best for your children."

Red Dove knew from the woman's blazing eyes that she had said much more. Finally, Old Tom jerked his head towards the wagon and climbed up onto the seat. Red Dove watched the woman tug on her heavy skirts and pull herself up next to him.

"You... must... go... to... school," she said, looking at Red Dove.

Must I? she wondered. Is that where I belong?

She had no more time to think before the white woman

grabbed the reins from Old Tom and steered the wagon through the trees, along the rutted path, and down to the meadow below.

≫ Just a Dream ≪

Sleep came slowly that night. Red Dove's worn old buffalo robe, usually a comfort, felt coarse and scratchy. She squirmed, rolling her body over to find a better position. There was something hard, a small round lump lodged beneath her, and no matter how much she twisted and turned, she couldn't avoid it.

My turtle amulet?

She sat up and reached under her robe. But this lump was rough and prickly, not smooth and regular like her mother's beaded gift. She held the thing up and squinted in the darkness.

With a rush of horror, she saw what it was:

The plum pit.

She closed her eyes and slumped back down.

I have to get rid of it.

Her mind raced, her body ached, and she was desperate for sleep. Instead, she lay awake, eyes wide, waiting for the smudge of light that would announce the dawn.

At last, when she thought she would never sleep again, she fell into a dream.

A white man's village, like the one she had visited the day before—crowded, noisy, and filled with people in Wasichu clothes— but not the heavy, round-limbed whites she knew. Instead, stick-like creatures with arms and legs of bleached-white bone. The men in long gray pants and coats, holding cross-covered books in their claw-like hands, their naked skulls rising out of stiff white collars and topped with bristly thatch. The women wearing lacy black headdresses, carrying baskets of bright red apples. The little ones scampering in short buttoned pants and frilly dresses hanging from skeleton bodies.

Red Dove, standing in the middle of the street, watching in terror, with no one noticing. How could they, with no eyes in their heads?

A voice: "Pick it up."

What?

"Pick it up."

Something lying there: pointed, sharp and small.

A plum pit.

Snatching it in panic, afraid to touch it, but more afraid not to. Holding it between her fingers, feeling its prickly surface, then closing her hand around it. And watching the skeleton bodies change.

Flesh growing on their limbs, covering them with pink, glowing skin. Long, narrow noses sprouting from their empty skulls and pale little eyes filling their sockets.

Turning together, towards her, circling closer.

"What do you want?"

The voice: "They cannot hear you, for they have no ears."

A scream.

Red Dove woke.

Was it me? Did I cry out? She looked at her family. All asleep. She pulled her robe close. Why did I dream that? What does it mean? The plum pit... I have to get rid of it.

She opened her fist, but it was empty. She searched her robe, the area around, but there was nothing there.

"Was it *all* just a dream?" she moaned.

›› Where I Belong ‹‹

"Walks Alone!" Red Dove yelled to her brother, who was sitting in the late afternoon shade of the little cottonwood tree. She had been waiting all day to talk with him. "Will the *Wasichu* give us food if we go to their school? Apples?"

"Why are you asking me, sister? You never take my advice."

That's because you never have much to give. "You know what their schools are like, from when you went to one before."

"It's where I learned not to trust white people," her brother snorted.

"So do they have the things she says?"

"Food you mean? They do, and they have warm places to sleep, and light you can carry around with you. They make marks on paper so their words will not be forgotten. But they do not honor them." He turned his clear-eyed gaze on her. "Yes, little sister, they have all that. But do you think they will share it with us?"

"I don't know—"

"Well *I* do. They won't. They'll only betray us like your father did."

"He was *your* father too," Red Dove said, stung by the blame in his words.

"He wasn't," said Walks Alone. "*My* father was Lakota. And he died at the hand of a white man."

Red Dove ducked her head. She knew this was a battle she wasn't going to win. She changed the subject. "That woman said she *wants* to help us."

"If we do what *she* wants."

"You mean go to school?"

Walks Alone narrowed his eyes. "*And* give up our ways, become like them."

"Is that so bad, if it means we'll get food?"

Walks Alone stared at his sister, as if seeing her for the first time. "It isn't right," he said.

"Why?"

"You shouldn't have to ask." He kicked at a clod of dirt at his feet. Then he raised his eyes to hers. "If you go to their school, they will steal your spirit, your power—"

"How?"

"They will beat it out of you—"

"No one would do that."

"Oh wouldn't they?" Walks Alone sneered. "Then go find out for yourself."

"Maybe I will," said Red Dove, shocked at the words coming out of her mouth.

"You wouldn't," her brother glared.

She glared back. "I would."

He rose, gave a dismissive wave, and stalked away.

He's wrong, Red Dove thought. It can't be like that. He was sick when he was there, so what does he know? I'm healthy… it'll be different for me.

But do I really want to?

And suddenly she did. Now the thought of going to the white man's school seemed like an adventure, a chance to prove herself to her family, to show that she could help—and make up for what she did .

She looked overhead at the patch of autumn blue sky framed by cottonwoods. *And* I'm half white. So maybe that woman was right. Maybe it is where I belong.

"Wake up, daughter." Falling Bird tugged on Red Dove's shoulder. "I've been up all night thinking," she murmured. "You and Walks Alone must go to the school. Today."

Squatting close to her, her mother whispered, "It's for the best... the best." Her arms were wrapped across her chest and her head was bowed.

Red Dove was fully awake now. "You said you didn't want me to. Does Grandfather think I should?"

"We'll talk as you get ready," Falling Bird pulled a deer bone comb through Red Dove's long black hair, plaiting it into two neat braids that fell behind her ears.

Alarm coursed through Red Dove. "Wait... ," she managed in a croaky whisper.

"You said that apple was delicious. And everyone knows how much you love to eat." Her mother tried to laugh. "The only way you'll get enough is if you go to the school."

"I don't want to," Red Dove blurted, and at that moment, she didn't. The plans she'd made the previous day seemed all wrong.

Falling Bird took her daughter's face in her hands. "There's no food for us here. You know that," she said as her voice started to break.

"But what about Walks Alone? Will he go too?"

"*Han.*"

"He won't. He hated it when he went to school before."

"He will have to—"

"And if he goes, who will do the hunting for you?"

"There isn't much game now and there won't be any once the snow sets in—"

"We always get by."

"We don't. And it will be even harder this winter. There aren't enough chokecherries and *timpsila* turnips to get us through."

"We can trade—"

"White people no longer want our beadwork." Her mother stared at the ground. "If you go, they will give us food."

"White people lie, you told me. Walks Alone says it too. Maybe they're lying this time."

"Maybe they are, but we have no choice." Falling Bird turned her face away. "I don't want to see you starve, Little One."

Little One—that's what she used to call me, thought Red Dove with a pang of sorrow so intense she wanted to cry out.

The choice wasn't hers to make. She *had* to go.

"You don't *want* me to leave, do you, Mother?"

"Leave?" Falling Bird choked. "I want you to stay, but you can't. Grandfather had a dream last night about what could happen."

"I had a dream, too," Red Dove said, but her mother didn't hear her.

"He saw soldiers on a hill," Falling Bird went on, "with guns so big they had to be carried on wagons. They were firing on a village—"

"Our village?"

"He didn't know. He thinks it was a warning. The whites take more and more and we can't stop them. They have weapons we don't—"

"Guns?"

"Yes, guns. And more. They have words and writing that

36

have power as well." Falling Bird fixed her eyes on Red Dove. "He thinks only *you* can help us. He thinks *you* are special."

Special? Red Dove looked away, not sure if what her mother said pleased or saddened her.

"You are young—young enough to learn their language and their writing. You can use their words *against* them and protect us from their tricks. Because you're clever." Falling Bird pulled something from out of her *parfleche*. "He wanted me to give you this."

Red Dove reached for the object. "A doll? He knows I'm too old—"

"He says it's for you to give to someone else," her mother said, "when the time is right. It will help you remember us and our ways, even as you learn the ways of the whites."

Red Dove stared at the blank, empty face of the doll, the beaded, red calico dress. She struggled against her tears as she saw the hopeful look on her mother's face. She forced a smile. "Thank you," she said, patting the soft calico. "It's beautiful. But don't tell me I have to go."

"You must, daughter. Today." Falling Bird rose slowly. "So we will get ready now. We will show the *Wasichu* how to behave. Come."

"But my coming of age—will I even have that?"

"I don't know, daughter. Now go say goodbye to your aunts and your cousins—"

Suddenly it was all too much. "No. And Walks Alone will never go!"

"He has no choice," said Falling Bird, her voice catching.

"And my cousins—"

"Will go when they are older."

Red Dove felt her heart tear in two. She wanted to scream; she wanted to run far, far away. She wanted to take that ugly old white woman, grab her by the shoulders and throttle her until—.

The night before, she had wanted to go—but now everything she had ever wished for was right here.

Her mother handed her a leather-wrapped bundle. "*Wasna* for the journey. I made it from the last of the venison and chokecherries."

"But they have food where I'm going, remember?"

"Take it anyway."

Red Dove reached for the little dried patty and with shaking fingers laid it in her *parfleche* bag. She tried, for one last time, to find a way to change her mother's mind. "Please don't make me leave," she begged.

"I'm sorry, daughter, but you must."

>> Special <<

"Come in, Granddaughter," called Gray Eagle as Red Dove walked slowly towards his lodge.

"You told Mother I had to go." She tried to keep her voice from breaking.

"This will be hard for you, and even harder for Falling Bird." Gray Eagle's face was creased with wrinkles and his tired old eyes were filled with worry. "The hurt is here; I know." He tapped his chest with gnarled old fingers.

"She said you had a dream. Well, I had one too," Red Dove blurted.

Gray Eagle nodded, as if he already knew. "Tell me."

"It's hard to explain."

"Try." He closed his eyes to listen.

"I was standing in the middle of a *Wasichu* town filled with people. They were skeletons, dressed like whites, moving around. Horrible. And as I watched, flesh grew on their bones and eyes filled the sockets in their heads—"

"They came back to life?"

"*Han*... as white people. I looked down and there, on the ground, was the plum pit—from the fruit I wasn't supposed to eat." She ducked her head to hide her embarrassment.

"*Hau*." The old man didn't open his eyes.

"And then I heard a voice. It told me to pick it up, but when I did, I woke."

Gray Eagle opened his eyes and gazed at the smoke hole above his head. He glanced down again. "The skeletons came back to life—but as white people? You're sure?"

Red Dove nodded. "Do you know what any of it means, Grandfather?"

"Maybe they are more powerful than I thought." He turned his gaze on her. "Have you ever heard of a man named *Wovoka*?"

Red Dove shook her head.

"He is a man from the west, a Paiute, and he had a dream like yours, but in his dream it was our people who came back from the dead." Gray Eagle stopped suddenly. "You are hungry to know things, Granddaughter." The lines in his face deepened with concern. "But you must wait for answers to come." He paused, took a deep breath and stirred the ashes of the cold fire. "So tell me now—what is it that you really want?"

"What I want?" For a moment, Red Dove didn't know.

And then she did. "I want people to hear me when I speak, Grandfather. I want them to listen... to what I say."

"And do they not?"

"No. They ignore me, as if I'm not important. As if I'm not even here."

Grandfather turned the ashes slowly with a stick and drew a circle in the dust. "You want the power to be heard. But why should they listen? Do you know so much more than they? What is it you would tell them, if you could?"

"Well," said Red Dove, suddenly unsure. "I... don't know."

"And what would you do with that power?" he asked.

"If I had that power, then I'm sure I would know what to do with it, Grandfather, because I would be wise—"

"Would you?" he asked, smiling broadly. "Power is given to many who are not—"

"But I would be, Grandfather," said Red Dove. "Wise. Like you." She held her breath, afraid she had said too much. And let it out when she saw the twinkle in his eyes.

"I see. Then you must learn to understand others first. You must hear what *they* hear, see what *they* see—and feel what *they* feel. You must know what is in their hearts. Here." He tapped his chest again. "You ask questions, Granddaughter, but do not hear the answers when they come. That is your flaw—"

"My flaw?"

"*Hau.* You know that the Great Spirit, *Wakan Tanka*, gave everyone a flaw, and that is the one he gave you—"

"Is that so terrible?"

"No." He smiled again. "Everyone has a flaw. It's what makes them special." He extended his hand. "Show me the doll your mother made."

Red Dove reached in her *parfleche* and gave it to him.

He held it up. "*Wakan Tanka* made each of us perfect, see? Like this little creature."

"She isn't perfect. She has no eyes, no nose, no mouth."

"That is so she won't think she's prettier, or better, than others. Now watch." He took his thumb, dipped it into the cold ash and pressed a smudge against the doll's blank face.

"Don't!" Red Dove cried.

"What do you think of her now?" he asked, handing it back.

"I think she's ugly. You've ruined her!"

"I haven't. Now she has a mark, a flaw, a place for spirit to enter, so she can understand the flaws—and the pain—of others."

Red Dove was on the verge of tears. "I don't understand," she moaned.

"You will, Granddaughter, when *Wakan Tanka* thinks the time is right—"

"But why can't I *now*?" A sudden thought occurred. "That's why I'm so different, isn't it, Grandfather? Because I'm not patient and I ask too many questions. That's why you're sending me away."

"That isn't it at all." The old man turned his head and she could no longer see the pain in his eyes. "You *do* belong here," he whispered. He stared up at the smoke that curled through the hole in the top of the lodge. "More than *anyone*, you belong here." He turned back again. "But you belong wherever you are. You are restless, a truth-seeker, a traveler between worlds. That is what makes you different, Granddaughter, and special—as are we all. You are like the bird I named you after—"

41

"A red dove?"

"The one I saw when I sat by myself at dawn, thinking about you and your brother and what your lives would be—"

"You called him Walks Alone."

"Because I knew he would choose to be by himself—"

"And then you saw the dove on a branch above your head. She was special, you said. Is it because of her color?" asked Red Dove, eager to hear more.

"The rose light of morning was on her wings—"

"So... she wasn't really red?"

"In the glow of dawn, she was—"

"Then she wasn't special at all. She was ordinary," said Red Dove, trying not to frown.

Gray Eagle ignored her disappointment. "She was ordinary and special. As ordinary as any creature—and as special. She sang to me but I knew her message was for you. She told me that you would live a life of great sadness and joy, that those feelings would give you your power, that you would share them with others, and that one day you would become—"

"*Iyeska*, you said. And travel between worlds."

>> The Pouch <<

The old man pulled out a small round object of dull gray leather. "Here," he said.

"An *opahte*?" Red Dove wrinkled her nose at the strange, musty smell.

"To make up for the one you lost—I know about that as well."

You know everything, Red Dove thought, so you probably know this is nothing like the amulet my mother gave me. That one was carefully worked, shaped like a turtle, and beaded in blue and yellow. This one is plain.

"*Pilamaya*," she said, bowing her head to hide her disappointment.

"Don't look so sad," Gray Eagle said. "Your old *opahte* contained the medicine that connected you to your mother and the earth. This one connects you to your power, so carry it always—but hidden, especially when you are with the *Wasichu*. And never, ever open it—"

"Why? What's inside?"

The old man shook his head. "That is not for you to know. It will connect you to your thoughts and feelings and to the thoughts and feelings of others. So never, *ever* use it in anger—or let it be used that way. Do you understand?"

"I'm not sure," said Red Dove.

"Hear me now, because there isn't much time. The power of the pouch will grow. It will open your ears and free your tongue, so you will speak the language of others—"

"I already do. I learned English listening to Walks Alone talking to Mother when he first came back from the school."

"You learned a few words. Now you must learn more. This will help you to do that, to listen and learn and communicate—"

"I'll understand white people?"

"And they will understand you. If you open your eyes and ears and watch their faces carefully, the thoughts behind their words will come clear—"

"I'll know what they're *thinking*?"

The old man nodded. "If you study them, you will know what they truly mean. And if you open your heart, you will feel what they feel."

Red Dove fingered the little bundle. "But it doesn't look like much, does it?"

"It is what you make it. Because its power comes from you. It will open you to dreams and visions, and give you answers you seek—and some you do not."

"Like the dream I told you about?"

"Like that, and like this." The old man pointed to the cold ashes. "See how it is?"

Red Dove wrinkled her brow and watched as the old man stirred the gray dust until the fire, dead until that moment, sprang to life.

"How did you do—"

"Look inside and see a story of your people."

Red Dove stared deep into the flames, and saw, dimly at first, a vision that began to form:

Gold seekers, white men shabby in denim and homespun, swarming into the sacred Black Hills, hungry for the yellow metal; others hunched over documents, quill pens in their hands, greedy for the precious land. Their angry voices warn her people's leaders that their families will starve unless they sign.

"We will not."

"Then we will find others who will, who can't read, who don't know what they're signing."

Grass-covered slopes and a pounding of hooves on earth. A yellow-haired soldier riding high into the hills... .

"The one is called Custer, coming for the gold—"

"Can't someone stop him, Grandfather?"

"Sitting Bull and Crazy Horse gathered warriors to do that, thousands of them, in the battle the *Wasichu* call Little Big Horn, the one we call the Greasy Grass—"

"We won, didn't we?"

"We did."

The yellow-haired general shakes his head, refusing to believe that thousands of Indians could mass against him and the blue-coated soldiers of the Seventh Cavalry. Gaily painted flags, a bugle call as the Yellow Hair waves his arm—

And then his terror, swift and sudden, as wave after wave of warriors, crying "Hoka Hey," storm the hill.

Peering through smoke and haze at the gaudy flags, lying crumpled in the dust, the bodies and the blood.

The vision shifts to blue-coated military men, swords at their sides and gold buttons flashing, mounting the steps of a white-columned building. They cross the hard marble floors and gather in a high-ceilinged room, as a man mounts a platform.

"It was a massacre," he cries. "Custer was outnumbered, so it wasn't fair—"

"But it was, wasn't it, Grandfather?"

"As fair as any battle. We had superior numbers so we won. That was what Sitting Bull tried to tell them, but the whites wouldn't listen. 'We did not go out of our own country to kill them,' he said. 'They came to kill us and got killed themselves. God so ordered it—'"

"So why didn't the *Wasichu* believe that?"

"They didn't want to. They made the Yellow Hair a martyr instead. 'We will avenge his death. We will avenge Custer's massacre at Little Big Horn.' And the plotting began."

"Plotting for what?"

There was a clatter from outside the tepee.

"Time is growing short, so take this and tie it around your neck. Quickly," Grandfather handed her the pouch.

Red Dove did, and as her fingers connected with the soft leather, her ears filled with a far-off buzzing, like a swarm of a thousand bees.

She dropped her fingers and the buzzing stopped. "Is that what the pouch can do?"

"The hiss of the rattle and the swarm of the hive," Grandfather whispered in her ear. "With it will come the words and thoughts of others, along with visions and dreams, as you have seen." He reached for a stick of sage, touched it to the glowing embers of the fire, and wafted a curl of smoke over Red Dove.

She opened her palms to gather the vapors that would soothe her spirit.

"Words carry medicine, Granddaughter. Remember that. And if you ever need my help, just ask. The pouch will connect us." He straightened stiffly off the ground.

"Always?" Red Dove whispered, rising slowly to meet him.

"*If* you find the courage to trust its power, it will." He placed a gentle hand on her shoulder. "So trust its power—and your own."

>> I Understand Her <<

The noise they'd heard came from the wagon, now waiting outside. Red Dove felt the weight in her chest as she watched the white woman climb down and walk towards the small group already gathered around the fire circle, all the people who remained in the village.

The woman saw Red Dove, and her frown changed to a smile. "Hello, my dear," she called brightly.

Red Dove didn't return her smile. Her heart hurt. A blunt, insistent ache lodged inside her and would not let go. It throbbed like the pain from the rock that hit her ankle that day in the *Wasichu* town.

I have to leave my home.

She touched the bundle around her neck and the strange noise, like a swarm of a thousand bees, began. She lowered her hand and the buzzing stopped. Grandfather said it would help me understand better. She raised her fingers again.

"Are you ready, my dear?" the woman was saying. "It's going to be a long journey and I want to make sure you're fully prepared."

Journey... prepared... I understand words I've never heard before. Is it because of the pouch? Red Dove dropped her hand and listened again, but with her fingers off the pouch, only a few words came clear.

She reached up once more.

"And now it's time to go to school," the woman said.

To school? Already? No!

Old Tom sat high in the wagon, whistling to himself and dangling the reins. He stared at the ground in front of the horses, his face covered by his crumpled hat.

Red Dove scanned the faces around the fire circle. Her anxious aunts held tight to her squirming cousins, who were still too small to be sent away. Her mother slumped next to Walks Alone, eyes to the ground. Grandfather stood apart, his expression blank.

The white woman jerked her head at Old Tom. "They don't understand me, Thomas, so you tell them."

"Sure thing, Sis," he answered.

But we *do* understand, thought Red Dove, fingers on the pouch, as she watched Old Tom hobble down off the seat. At least I do. Every word.

The woman took a step closer to Red Dove and held out the flat, black book with the cross on the cover.

She said it was a Bible. It looks like the one the skeletons were carrying in my dream.

"Inside this, you will find all of the answers to all of your questions," the woman said.

Red Dove expected the woman to hand it to her, but instead she jerked it back and shoved it into the satchel. "Later. After you've learned to read. First this." She pulled out a small round package, wrapped in white paper.

An apple?

Red Dove stepped forward to take it, just as the woman snatched it away. Smiling coyly, she unwrapped the paper, raised the shiny ripe fruit to her lips and took a tiny bite. She held it up. "See? Outside, red, but inside white… like you with your strange gray eyes, my dear."

Red Dove looked at the pink-faced woman, the apple in her hand. Then she looked at her mother's ashen face.

Tell me what to do, Mother, because I don't know!

Suddenly she did know, and her legs carried her around the fire circle, away from the white people and towards Gray Eagle. "I won't go," she said.

"You must."

"Come back here, you," said the woman, dropping the apple. She moved slowly towards her.

Red Dove grabbed her grandfather's fingers with one hand and the pouch with the other. "I won't," she repeated.

"*You must, you must, you must,*" she heard through the din of a thousand bees.

Red Dove looked at the apple, lying half-bitten in the dust. "Take it, Mother," she whispered, raising her eyes to meet those of Falling Bird.

It is not for us, her mother seemed to say. "*Toksa,*" she heard her mother whisper. "We will meet again."

She looked at her grandfather and the faces all around. She saw the resignation that they wore.

At that moment, Red Dove knew she had no choice. The adults she loved could no longer protect her. She was on her own.

She gripped her grandfather's hand as tightly as she could. She felt its delicate thinness, its gentle heat, the papery softness of his fingers.

And finally let go.

>> Civilized <<

The wagon clattered over the bumpy, rutted road. From their perch facing backward, Red Dove and Walks Alone watched their old life disappear as the landscape changed from pinkish bluffs and evergreen hills to open prairie clotted with grass and scrub. The air was thick with the scent of sage mingled with dirt and dust. Red Dove had been here before during her family's long wanderings, but now everything looked strange.

"Not been introduced—" Red Dove heard Jerusha say.

What? Red Dove turned around to see Jerusha point to herself. She touched the pouch and the meaning became clear.

"Not properly, that is." Jerusha fixed Red Dove with her bright, birdlike gaze. She waved at Old Tom beside her. "This is my brother, Thomas. Some call him Old Tom but you should call him Mr. Kincaide—"

"Just call me Tom."

"Oh, all right." Jerusha frowned. "Everything here is so informal. You can call me Jerusha."

"Je—" Red Dove started, but didn't finish, as Jerusha filled the air with her chatter and Red Dove tired of listening. She took her eyes off the woman, dropped her hand from the pouch and the words became nonsense again.

Walks Alone, shoulders slumped, stared back at the disappearing landscape.

What's *he* thinking? She had seen the anguish in his face when he climbed onto the wagon. This is *your* fault, it seemed to say.

·Is it?

The sun crested as they rode, lighting the dusty trail, until finally, the broad, angular buildings of a white man's town came into view.

Old Tom brought the wagon to a halt and muttered something.

Red Dove touched her pouch and watched, listening.

Old Tom dropped from the wagon and started towards two swinging doors marked *SALOON*.

"Wait. Where are you going, Thomas?" said Jerusha, looking anxiously around. "You can't just leave us here."

Old Tom just kept walking.

"He's getting directions to the school, probably," said Jerusha, shading her eyes as she watched him disappear inside the building. She pulled a piece of ivory cloth out of her satchel and dabbed at her neck and forehead.

Red Dove looked at the ramshackle buildings, some painted, most left a weathered gray. What's inside? she wondered, but the cracked glass in the few small windows was too murky to see through.

"Come away, Abigail!" a woman screeched, breaking her thoughts.

Red Dove touched her pouch and stared. The woman wore a lacy bonnet and was tugging on a round-faced little girl in a frilly yellow dress. Next to her was a boy in suspenders and short pants that reached his scabby knees.

They're dressed like the people in my dream.

The girl gazed wide-eyed at Red Dove. She pulled something from her mouth and held it out.

"Don't give her your candy. No!" The woman swatted it from the girl's hand.

The girl stared at the fallen candy, lying sticky in the dirt. Then she looked up at Red Dove and began to wail.

"Indians," muttered the woman, dragging both children into one of the shops. "Come away!"

Jerusha clucked in disapproval. "Some people have no manners."

They hate us. Why?

Red Dove's fingers searched the bottom of the *parfleche* until she found what she was looking for: the black leather-bound book that Jerusha told them held all the answers. She opened it.

"Well now," said Jerusha with a shy smile. "Would you like me to read it to you, my dear?"

Red Dove nodded.

"It will make the time pass more quickly. But let's wait

until Thomas gets back, so he can translate any words you don't understand—"

"I *do* understand," said Red Dove in a clear, strong voice, her fingers touching the pouch.

"Where did you learn English?" asked Jerusha.

"From my brother and mother. They lived with my father. A white man. But I don't remember much. At least I thought I didn't. Maybe it's because of this—" She patted the top of her deerskin robe—then remembered her grandfather's warning and dropped her hand.

Jerusha waved at a fly buzzing around her nose and wiped her shining forehead. "What is it you have there, under your collar?"

"Nothing."

"Then why do you keep touching your neck? Are you hiding something? Let me have a look."

Red Dove pulled back. "*Hiya!*" she shouted. "No!"

"Well, honestly. I just wanted to help—"

"Good," blurted Red Dove, desperate for a way to change the subject. "*Washte.* I help you too. I teach our language."

Jerusha laughed. "You want me to learn *your* language? Why should I do that?"

"So we… can talk."

"We're talking now, aren't we?" Jerusha pressed her lips together. "Look, my dear, it's important that you learn *our* language, so you can be civilized—"

"Civilized?"

"Yes. Learn to be like us."

"White people?"

"Of course," said Jerusha. "But we'll discuss that later.

Right now I'd better go see what's keeping Thomas." She stepped carefully off the wagon, down onto the street and started walking towards the saloon. "Thomas?" Red Dove heard her call as the doors swung closed behind her.

Grateful for a moment of quiet, Red Dove looked around at the dusty street, her brother now dozing beside her. She thought about the angry woman and remembered the venom in her words.

Is that what it means to be civilized?

>> Delicious <<

Red Dove waited, eyes fixed on the hanging doors of the saloon. Another drop of sweat rolled down her neck. She brushed it away and felt the pressure in her bladder.

Her thoughts began to drift.

She saw a shape lean up against a building. It was the same boy she had seen before, but his mother and sister were gone. Brown-haired and scrawny, the boy looked half her age. He was holding a plum: ripe, purple, and heavy with juice.

"Delicious," she murmured, wishing she could taste it. She touched her fingers to the pouch and watched him bite down.

A burst of flavor exploded on her tongue and a lush sweetness filled her mouth. She felt her teeth break through the crisp skin to the fleshy meat as juice tickled her chin. Now she was chewing, swallowing, sucking on the small, scratchy seed until every morsel was gone.

Is this what Grandfather said would happen? He said the pouch would open me to dreams and visions, that I would understand people's words—and feel what they feel. Is this what he meant? Or am I just dreaming?

Out of the corner of her eye, Red Dove saw someone come out of a shop.

"You've made a mess again, Harold," the woman shouted, raising her hand above the boy.

Don't!

Red Dove dropped her fingers from the pouch as the hand smacked down—but not soon enough. The slap fell hard and she felt the sting.

"Aiyeee!" She jumped.

"Sister?" Walks Alone startled awake. "What's wrong?"

"Nothing." Stunned and confused, Red Dove touched her fingers to her burning cheek. "I… must have had a dream. But it felt so real."

>> I've Come to Help <<

Sweating in her deerskin dress, Red Dove felt her exhaustion. Her arms were sticky, now coated with the sweat and grime kicked up by horses' hooves. She longed for the coolness of the stream that flowed through their village, the one where she used to swim.

Used to, she thought.

"We're back," Jerusha announced, clambering into the wagon.

Old Tom lumbered up behind and Red Dove smelled the sick-sweet stink of whisky as he jerked the reins and they all lurched forward.

"Did you get directions to the school?" Jerusha asked over the clatter of the wheels.

"Yeah, Sis," Old Tom mumbled.

"Well, then tell us where you're taking us, Thomas. We're

hot, we're thirsty and we're so tired, so please say you know where we're going—"

"Five miles yonder, that direction." Old Tom nodded at the road ahead.

"Is that what they told you in there?"

"Nope. Knew it all along. Been there before."

"You have? Why didn't you say so?"

"Like to keep you guessin', Sis," Old Tom said, as a faint smile curled the corner of his mouth. "You're always so darn sure of everythin'."

Jerusha didn't answer. Instead, she sat rigid with annoyance, staring straight ahead.

He's not very nice to her, Red Dove thought. She says she's come to help us, but what does that mean? Fingers on the pouch, she twisted her head to stare at Jerusha's rounded back.

"What is it you're plannin' to do, Sis?" said Old Tom, asking the question for her.

"Help these people. If that's what God wants, I'll wait for instructions. I've been meaning to ask you... that medicine man—"

"Gray Eagle? The *wicasa wakan?*"

She's talking about Grandfather . . .

"Shhh," Jerusha warned. "Keep your voice down or they'll hear us."

"Can't. They're sleepin'," said Old Tom.

I'm not, thought Red Dove. I'm just pretending to be.

"You said his people think he's a magician—"

"A shaman. He has powers."

"Powers? Why, Thomas, that's absurd. What can he do?"

Old Tom was silent for a moment. "You saw him disappear," he said at last.

"That was just a silly trick—"

"Weren't no trick, Sis."

It wasn't! Red Dove wanted to shout. He *does* have powers. He healed my brother when he was sick with fever. He gave him his spirit back again. And he gave me the pouch!

"His people believe in him and they listen to him, more'n they'll listen to me or you. They been tricked an' lied to by white folks, time an' time again. Know what they call us?" He didn't wait for an answer. "*Wasichu*. Means the ones that take the fat, the best part of the meat. That's how they see us, helpin' ourselves to what we want."

"Why Thomas, you're not making any sense. You've been here so long—maybe too long. I've always meant to ask, why did you leave your life back East?"

"Dunno, Sis. Can't rightly say. Guess I just wanted somethin' more... but what about you? Why are you here?"

"I suppose I wanted something more as well."

Red Dove, peering round, was surprised to see Old Tom place his hand gently on Jerusha's. "Must'a been kind hard for you back there."

"Oh, Thomas," choked Jerusha, raising her handkerchief to her lips. "Why did they all have to go?"

Old Tom patted Jerusha's hand. "Parents die, Jerusha. It's the natural course of things—"

"Yes, but losing them both at once. And then my fiancé—"

"Who? Oh yeah, forgot about that. You were s'posed to marry him, weren't you?" Old Tom pulled on his hat brim.

"Guess you've had a pretty rough time of it, haven't you, Sis? Well, you'll find somethin' here to make up for it all."

"Will I, Thomas? The missionaries seem to think so, but I don't know," said Jerusha with a sigh.

"Sure you will, Jerusha." Old Tom cocked his head.

Jerusha shifted sideways to stare at the vast, empty prairie far in the distance. "I suppose you're right, Thomas. Maybe this isn't like the person I used to be. Maybe I'm becoming a whole new person, with a whole new life."

>> Ghost Dance <<

"Do you hear that?"

Walks Alone's urgent whisper startled Red Dove awake. She saw where she was, slumped against his shoulder on the rocking wagon, her hand wedged between her chin and neck, fingers touching the pouch. The air was cooler now, the sun lower in a cloudless sky.

"What's that over yonder?" Old Tom wondered, squinting past the thicket of trees that lined the road.

Jerusha shaded her eyes and looked to where her brother was pointing. "There is something, isn't there... what? Smoke?"

"Nope. Dust, I reckon—"

"And that noise. Sounds like thunder."

"Ain't thunder—"

"*Isn't*, Thomas, the word is *isn't*. What on earth could it be?" Jerusha squinted against the late-day glare.

"*Wanagi Wachi*," said Walks Alone. Red Dove saw the excitement in his eyes as he craned around.

"What's that?" asked Jerusha.

"Ghost Dance," Old Tom answered.

"Really? I'd like to watch. Please stop the wagon—"

"Ain't regular dancin', Sis. Some white folks think it's more like a war dance. Could be dangerous—"

"Dancing? Nonsense. Please stop. How am I going to help these people unless I learn more about them?" She nodded at a craggy boulder to her right. "I'll head up there so they won't see me."

"I don't think—"

"I'll be careful," Jerusha said matter-of-factly. "Do as I ask, please.

Old Tom shook his head and brought the wagon to a halt and Jerusha climbed down. "You stay here and guard the children," she said, before picking up her skirts and making her way slowly up the boulder, slipping and sliding in her leather-soled shoes.

"Dang woman. Won't listen to anyone or anythin'," Old Tom mumbled as he flicked the reins against his knee and sighed. He shook his head, pulled his hat down low over his eyes, and slumped back on the wagon bench. "Dang woman," he repeated, before he fell into a deep doze and began to snore.

Walks Alone put a finger to his lips.

"What are you doing?" Red Dove whispered.

Her brother pointed to the fringe of cottonwoods. "The Ghost Dance," he said. "Wait here."

Walks Alone slipped off the wagon and raced across the open field towards the trees.

Red Dove stared at his departing back. "Don't leave me," she whispered, and waited, watching the wind riffle the sea of grass between her and the line of trees.

I'm not waiting any more, she thought and climbed quietly down to follow her brother. The steady roar grew louder as she approached, until at last she saw the source of the sound: a vast encampment of hide-covered tepees arranged in an enormous circle. In the center were throngs of men, women and children, more than she had ever seen in her life, chanting and swirling in a dizzying dance.

She didn't see Walks Alone, huddled behind a downed cottonwood, until she almost toppled over him. "Watch out!" he called.

She crouched low. "Who are they? What are they doing?" She struggled to be heard above the din.

"What does it look like? Dancing. It's what *Wovoka*, the Paiute, said they should do—"

"Grandfather told me."

Walks Alone sighed. "If he told you, why are you asking?"

"I want to know more. Tell me about the prophecy."

Her brother rolled his eyes. "I will if you stop interrupting." Speaking more loudly now, confident that they could not be heard by the dancers, he went on. "*Wovoka* dreamed that the whites would drown in a giant flood and that the buffalo would return, that flesh would cover the bones of the dead—"

"The *Wasichu* dead?" Red Dove asked, remembering her dream of blue-white skin covering bleached white bone.

"*Our* dead, sister." Walks Alone smiled. "*Wovoka* dreamed that *our* people would regain the earth. But only if we danced and danced and never stopped."

Red Dove caught sight of a warrior in a tunic painted the color of the sky and covered with stars and turtles and fantastic shapes. "What's he wearing?"

"A medicine shirt to protect him from white man's bullets," Walks Alone said. "To keep him safe."

"Safe from bullets? Then why don't our people do that? Why don't they dance and dance and wear the painted shirts?"

"Grandfather thinks it will scare the whites and just make things worse for us—"

"Do you believe that?"

"I don't know," her brother said. "Sometimes I think Grandfather's wrong, that he's just an old man—"

Just an old man? Grandfather? Red Dove stared at her brother, shocked that he could say such a thing.

Walks Alone caught her glance and tilted his head. "Things are changing, little sister. Grandfather doesn't always know what our people need now."

He *does*. He's Grandfather! But Red Dove didn't voice her thoughts. "What is it our people need, brother?" she asked instead.

"Guns," said Walks Alone, turning away.

Red Dove watched a woman, far across the circle, about her mother's age, tap the ground lightly with her feet and sway. But something was wrong. Her steps were slowing, as she lost time with the music and fell.

"Help her," Red Dove said, but Walks Alone didn't respond. His eyes were fixed on a group of male dancers pounding the earth in front of them and the drumming was so loud he didn't hear. "Well if you won't, I will," she said, and hoisted herself over the log barrier between them and the dancers.

Walks Alone grabbed her hem and pulled her back. "Don't!"

"But she's fallen—"

"She's doing what she's supposed to do, dancing until she falls into a trance." He gazed at Red Dove with his steady dark eyes. "Don't you understand? It's part of the prophecy."

"It is?" Red Dove stared at the fallen woman, the people swirling around her, treading gently, careful not to disturb her trance, and dancing until they too fell to the ground.

"I should be with them," she heard her brother say.

"No, you shouldn't. Grandfather wouldn't like it."

"It doesn't matter what he thinks—"

It doesn't?

Red Dove looked up at her brother's handsome profile, his sharp, even features, the lock of thick black hair that fell across his forehead. And then she asked the question that was burning inside, now that everything seemed to be changing. "You do still care about me, don't you, brother? We'll stay together, won't we?"

"Of course—"

"*There* you are!" Jerusha screeched, grabbing Red Dove and pulling her up. "I've been looking all over. Come. Quickly!" She tugged on Red Dove's sleeve and pulled her up and away.

Red Dove looked back at her brother, saw his anguished face as he gazed first at her and then back at the dancers. She watched him turn, shrug, and numbly follow across the field and up to the wagon.

Yes, little sister, he seemed to say, I *do* care about you. And this is how I show it.

Chanwape Kasna Wi

The Moon-of-Falling-Leaves

Mission Boarding School

The Reservation—Early Fall, 1890

» I'm Sister Agatha «

The sun sank low behind the hills, the air carried a chill, and the sky shimmered from gold to pink to purple-gray, as they covered the miles between them and the school. Red Dove shifted on the hard wagon bench, avoiding the rough splinters that threatened her robe while she watched her world disappear.

She looked at her brother dozing beside her, his head slumped on his chest.

He wanted to run away. Why? What's he so afraid of? What does he know that I don't? "Walks Alone?" she whispered, but he didn't answer.

I have other ways to find out, she thought, touching her fingers lightly to the pouch, just as the wagon jerked to a stop.

"We're here," Jerusha announced. "The school."

Red Dove felt her stomach lurch and craned her neck to see where they were. Against the dimming light, there before them loomed a building. High walls rose up from the earth, pierced by rows of tiny windows, right angles of black against blood-red brick. Beneath a thin white spire topped with a cross that perched above the roof, a massive oak door sat closed but waiting.

"You sure you want to do this, Sis? Somethin' don't smell right to me," Old Tom mumbled.

"*Doesn't*, Thomas. The word is *doesn't*. How many times do I have to tell you?"

The door creaked open before Jerusha could finish her sentence and a tall, gaunt woman in a long, dark gown appeared. Her hair was covered by a thick black veil. Her pale, narrow face was framed by a band of white that wrapped her forehead, shrouded her chin and covered her chest. A string of thick brown beads dangled from her waist. She raised a wrinkled hand in greeting, then buried it again beneath the folds of blue fabric that hung like a banner to the ground. And waited, motionless.

"Is this the school?" Jerusha asked with a note of hesitation in her voice.

"Yes," said the woman, through thin, chapped lips.

"We've brought them—the children."

"Children?" said the woman with a frown.

Red Dove sensed Jerusha's anxiety. "The ones I wrote about in my letter. Didn't you get it?" Jerusha asked in a voice pitched slightly too high. "I explained that I was bringing them and that I was available to come and teach. The missionaries made all the arrangements."

"I never got it." The woman's cold, pale eyes fell on them. A shiver ran through Red Dove.

"Maybe it got lost en route," said Jerusha tentatively.

"No matter," said the woman. "We'll find room."

"But... the arrangements, my offer to teach. We need to discuss—"

"We'll find room for *them*, I said." The strange woman strode up to the wagon, robes swishing as she walked. She extended her thin, narrow hand. "I'm Sister Agatha."

Jerusha hesitated. "Sister—"

"Agatha."

"But... you're Irish. Judging from your accent—" Jerusha said, looking nervously around.

"What was it you were expecting?" said the woman, lowering her hand and hiding it beneath her robe.

"They told me the nuns here were German—"

"Reverend Mother and most of the rest... but some of us aren't. I hope that won't be a problem," Sister Agatha narrowed her eyes.

"Why no... of course not." Jerusha, totally flustered now, dabbed at her neck with the wadded handkerchief. "I didn't mean... It's just that the Catholics I'm used to are German, more like us Protestants." She smiled weakly.

Sister Agatha ignored her and crossed to the back of the wagon, pulling her long-sleeved arm from beneath her robe and motioning for Red Dove and Walks Alone to get down.

"It *has* been a long journey," Red Dove heard Jerusha say,

"and we're all so bone-weary tired. So come along, children. Let's go and see where you'll be staying," she said, trying to sound cheerful.

Red Dove heard the creak of wood and metal as Jerusha lowered herself off the wagon, but her eyes were still fixed on the terrifying woman. Finally, with one hand on the pouch and the other gripping her *parfleche*, Red Dove climbed down.

Sister Agatha put up a hand to stop her. "Let me get a good look at you first," she said, pinching Red Dove's thin arm with her bony fingers.

"Underfed," the nun said, propelling Red Dove towards the door. "Thought as much. Go inside."

"Maybe now you'll get some food, children," said Jerusha, hopefully. "Let's go and see—"

"Not you," said Sister Agatha.

"What?"

"They're my business now," the nun called over her shoulder.

"But—" Jerusha, still standing by the wagon, looked helplessly at Old Tom.

"Better this way." Sister Agatha marched up to the door and threw it wide. "Come on!"

Red Dove looked from Jerusha to Old Tom to her brother, who was now climbing slowly off the wagon.

"I think it *is* better this way, children... isn't it?" said Jerusha, too brightly.

She wants *us* to reassure *her*, Red Dove thought. She watched Walks Alone cross the gravel courtyard, shoulders slumped, eyes down, as he marked the steps towards his fate. Together they mounted the high threshold into the dark, narrow hall.

"That nun's crazy," she heard Old Tom say, before the door closed firmly behind them.

≫ You Won't Be Seeing Him Again ≪

The night was cool, but the air inside was colder still. The glass windows were draped, blocking any daylight that remained. Smooth, flat walls rose steeply from the floor and reflected the glare of foul-smelling lamps. Sister Agatha's footsteps echoed on the hard, polished tile, so different from the soft, packed earth of Red Dove's village.

"Hurry," the nun said, barreling through yet another door and over an even higher threshold. It was darker by the moment now and harder to see as Sister Agatha's heavy footfalls marked their progress, *clomp, clomp, clomp,* until finally they came to a narrow passage leading up. "Mind the stairs. They're steep."

Stairs, thought Red Dove as they climbed, feeling the evenness of boards beneath her feet.

They reached the top and faced yet another hallway, lit by a single glowing lamp. She could just make out a framed picture of light-skinned men and women in long, white robes, heads circled in gold.

Who are they? she wondered as they reached the end of the hall.

Sister Agatha creaked open yet another door. "In here," she muttered. Her clawlike fingers dug into Walks Alone's chest, pushing him back behind the threshold. "Just her. Come on."

Walks Alone! Red Dove wanted to cry out.

He stood silent, watchful, nodding slightly. Go ahead, sister, he seemed to say as the door closed between them.

Moving slowly, Red Dove followed the nun into the room.

The nun walked up to a small table, picked up a stick and rubbed it against a piece of rough paper. Red Dove heard a scratch, a hiss and a blue and yellow flame burst from the end.

"Matches," Sister Agatha muttered, answering her thoughts. "Some people call them Lucifers. Name of the Devil." Holding the match upright, she touched it to a thin cord that dangled from a tall glass tube filled with murky yellow liquid, and the room burst into light.

Red Dove blinked and looked around. Her eyes stung from the brightness and the smoke. She wrinkled her nose.

"Kerosene. You'll get used to it. Look over there. Your bed."

Red Dove squinted past the rows and rows of metal frames covered with dull gray blankets to the far end of the room.

My bed?

She moved closer to get a better look. Something was hanging on the wall above it: a tiny, near-naked man, wearing only a breechcloth, hands and feet nailed to two crossed beams, eyes raised in agony. She jumped back.

"Stupid girl!" Sister Agatha barked. "Haven't you never seen a crucifix before?

Sister Agatha nodded at a small chest next to the bed. "Clothes are in there. A dress, pinafore, everything you'll need. May be too big, but they'll have to do. So go ahead, get ready for supper... busy... things to do... didn't know you were coming."

The nun was barking out instructions so fast, Red Dove could hardly keep up. Then she said words Red Dove understood clearly:

"Leave your old things on the floor so we can throw 'em out in the morning. And I'll be taking the lamp with me now," said the nun. "Sure, you've enough light for your young eyes."

Red Dove wheeled around, wanting to see her brother before the light was gone.

Sister Agatha opened the door. He wasn't there.

"Where did he go?" Red Dove gasped.

"Your brother?" Surely you didn't think we'd let you stay together now, did you?" she said, raising her pale brows and laughing. "He's gone to the priests like all the other boys. So you won't be seeing him again."

The door closed behind her, darkness filled the room, and Red Dove, unable to bear any more, at last gave in to tears.

>> Pass the Bread <<

Feeling her way through the gloom the nun left behind, Red Dove opened the rough wood chest and pulled out the first thing she touched. "Dress," she whispered. Even in the dim light, she could tell the musty cloth was gray. She laid her deerskin robe carefully on the bed. Dragging the thin fabric over her head, she poked her neck up and through. Reaching back, she felt a row of openings opposite a line of tiny, pebble-like beads. They were meant to connect somehow, she knew, but even twisting and turning, she couldn't fasten them all.

She opened the chest again. Lying inside, just visible against the darkness, was a piece of white ruffled cotton. "Pinafore," the nun had said. She wrapped it around her front and tied the loose bow in back. Then she pulled on the scratchy wool socks, forced her still-sore ankle into one of the boots and looked at the tangle of laces. "I'll tie them later," she mumbled, as she stuffed her foot into the other boot.

Then she felt for the soft deerskin lying on the bed.

I won't let them throw my clothes away!

She reached under and felt along a crack in the floor.

Something's loose... . She tugged gently and the board gave with a creak. Pulling harder, her fingers searched the gap.

It's big enough.

She pushed the deerskin inside and saw something else lying underneath the bed.

My pouch! It fell off while I was dressing!

She grabbed it and thrust it in her pocket. She then followed the sound of voices down the steep, narrow steps. She walked along the corridor towards the murmurs of young voices coming from an enormous, brightly lit room at the end. It was filled with rows of rough, wooden tables flanked by benches. On the benches sat dozens of girls—all staring back at her.

Like me... but different.

Their skin was brown, their eyes were dark, but their black, glossy hair was chopped to the line of the chin.

Their braids are gone... are they in mourning?

She watched their faces.

They don't seem friendly... are they smiling... or laughing at me?

She listened to the whispered English that filled the room and, hand in her pocket, she felt for the pouch.

A rush of sound overwhelmed her, first a hissing drone, then a jumble of strange new words as she peered at face after face, hoping to understand—but the tangle of thoughts confused her. *"What's wrong with her eyes? They're strange... gray... not like ours."*

She whirled around—and thudded straight into Sister Agatha.

"Watch it!"

Frightened gasps filled the room.

"Silence!" roared Sister Agatha.

Dozens of dark, frightened eyes turned towards the nun.

"Miriam," Sister Agatha called. "Come here, child."

A pretty, sharp-chinned girl rose with a smirk and sauntered up to Red Dove.

"This is Mary," said Sister Agatha, pointing at Red Dove.

That's not my name!

"Hello, Mary," Miriam said in a voice of milky sweetness.

"She will need a *lot* of help, as you can see. Since you're older'n she is, I'd like you to look after her."

"Yes, Sister," said Miriam.

"I knew I could rely on you." Sister Agatha clapped her hands together. "And you, Mary, take your hand out of your pocket. That's a nasty habit."

Red Dove pulled out her hand as Miriam returned to her seat and the rest of the girls resumed their careful whispering.

Red Dove stood awkwardly, not knowing what to do. She strained her ears, longing for the comfort of her language. Surely someone here speaks it, she thought.

But all she heard was the hard-edged language of the *Wasichu*. In her confusion and not finding a friendly face to focus on, she couldn't understand a word.

I *do* need the pouch, she thought... but didn't dare reach for it.

Miriam pointed to the seat next to her. "Sit," she hissed.

Red Dove sat down across from a tiny girl whose bright, dark eyes glowed up at her.

"Hannah," said the little girl, pointing to herself.

"Red Dove, *Wakiyela Sa*—"

"You're Mary," said Miriam. "So get used to it."

Mary? Red Dove wondered again. Why?

When she thought no one was looking, she reached into her pocket. Her fingers lightly grazed the pouch as she watched the faces around her.

And understood.

They're not really laughing at me. They just don't know what else to do, because they're sad, too—very sad. They're each remembering the day *they* arrived here, what it's been like since. Even Miriam, she realized.

Wedged up next to her, Red Dove watched the other girls sitting on benches, shoulders hunched and staring ahead as they waited.

For what?

On some signal she failed to see, the girls folded their hands and closed their eyes, murmuring in unison. Red Dove bowed her own head, trying to make sense of what they were chanting.

And then, more silence.

Red Dove waited until finally Sister Agatha said something—*Amen*, was it? She opened her eyes just as an elbow jabbed her ribs.

"Pass the bread," said Miriam, pointing at the wooden bowl that held a dried-out loaf.

Red Dove did and Miriam broke off a piece. She pushed the bowl far from Red Dove.

When Miriam wasn't looking, Hannah pushed it back.

"*Wopila*," Red Dove managed before a slap sent the loaf flying.

"The word is 'thank you,' miss," growled a fat, greasy-faced nun, her hand still in the air. "Don't let me hear zat heazen talk coming out your mouze or I vill shove a bar of soap in it."

Tears blurred Red Dove's vision. She stared at her plate, took a breath and waited. Finally, she picked up a chunk of potato in the bowl next to her plate and raised it to her mouth.

This time the slap came down on the side of her head. "Stupid girl!" the nun screeched, as the potato broke into a floury mass on her plate. "Use a fork!"

Fork?

Hannah pointed to a pronged metal implement lying by her plate and Red Dove reached for it, but her hand was shaking so much she couldn't raise it to her mouth.

What now? she wondered sadly, as she looked at the girls around her, quietly eating.

Tomorrow then, I'll eat tomorrow, she decided, and dropped her hand back down.

Little Hannah caught her eye. She picked up a piece of bread, put it in her pocket and smiled. I'll save it for you, she seemed to say.

>> The Scent of Sun-Drenched Pines <<

The meal over, Red Dove followed the girls out of the dining hall, up the stairs and into the vast dormitory. She sat on her bed, and with her back to the room, reached in her pocket, and tried to tie the pouch around her neck.

"What's that?" Miriam said from the bed behind her.

Red Dove dropped her hand. "My *opahte*—"

"Use English! The nuns'll take it away if they see it. But if you're lucky, we won't tell, will we?" Miriam said with a wicked grin.

Will they? wondered Red Dove, searching the faces of the girls around.

"Prayer time," Miriam announced, folding her hands and dropping to her knees beside the bed. "You too," she nodded at Red Dove. "Hail Mary, full of grace, the Lord is with thee."

Red Dove knelt, closed her eyes and waited while the rough floorboards dug into her knees.

The door creaked open. She opened her eyes and saw Sister Agatha. "Sayin' your rosaries? Good night then, girls."

"Good night, Sister Agatha," the girls chimed back.

The door shut. Beds creaked and floorboards groaned before the room went quiet. Someone walked over to the lamp, blew it out, and all went black.

Red Dove listened to the sounds of sleep, waiting. With the door shut, the place was hot and stuffy and airless. Through the clouded pane of the tiny casement window, she could just make out some starry shapes. *Wichinchala Sakowin*—the seven little girls carried to the sky by an eagle, a story from the Cheyenne people that Grandfather used to tell. They're with me now, even here.

Then, from far outside, she heard another sound, a comforting coo, a five-note trill.

But doves don't fly at night, do they?

She fell into a dream before she could think of an answer.

Drifting high above the room of sleeping girls. Floating free of the dark dormitory and over a place she knew, her people's home, the Black Hills—the beloved Paha Sapa. *Smelling clover-scented air; seeing rivers dancing in the mist; granite crags thrusting up; buffalo so plentiful they churn a sea of yellow grass to black.*

"Gray Eyes; remember why you are here: to listen and to learn."

I will, Grandfather, Red Dove murmured. *She saw his kindly old face before it began to blur.*

Grandfather?

"Enough for now." The words began to fade.

"Grandfather?" Red Dove tried again, but the vision disappeared.

She opened her eyes. Light seeped through the cloudy pane as dawn approached and the air carried a chill. She looked at the girls sleeping round her, pulled the blanket close and shut her eyes again, longing for the world of dreams that she had left.

A door creak woke her and she squinted at the morning light. The room was empty, the girls gone.

No!

Little Hannah walked over to her, holding out a piece of bread. "Here," she said. "Miriam say not wake you... but I know you hungry." Her bright eyes shone down at Red Dove.

"*Wopila*—I mean, thank you."

"You late. Hurry to chapel," Hannah laid the bread carefully on Red Dove's rumpled blanket and scurried from the room.

Red Dove tore off her nightgown, pulled the starchy gray dress off its hanger and tugged it over her head. She quickly finished dressing and made her way down the stairs.

The hall was empty.

Panic gripped her.

"Where are they?"

She looked through the open door to the courtyard and saw them all heading back into the building.

>> Was It Something You Were Forgetting? <<

Is that the chapel Hannah talked about? Red Dove was about to step out onto the gravel courtyard when she heard the sound of women's voices coming through a half-opened door behind her. She looked in the room and saw Jerusha sitting at a table, rubbing her temples. Standing over Jerusha was the well-fed nun who had slapped Red Dove.

Red Dove ducked behind the half-closed door and peered through the crack between the door and the wall.

"Sister Agatha vil be mit you in a minute," Red Dove heard the nun say.

Jerusha raised her head. "Yes, thank you, Sister... ?"

"Gertrude."

"Are the children all right? I worry about them."

Red Dove wedged herself tighter into the space to hear the answer. She reached up to touch the pouch and sighed with relief to find it still tied around her neck.

"Vich children?"

"The ones I brought, of course," said Jerusha, frowning. "Red Dove and her brother Walks Alone—"

"Ach, Mary und George—"

"You renamed them?" Jerusha raised an eyebrow.

"Mit proper Christian names. Zey get used to it, like ze rest."

"Where is Mary, then?"

Here! Red Dove wanted to shout—but didn't.

"What's this?" barked Sister Agatha, coming from the other end of the hall.

Oh no, she saw me! What'll she do? A chill ran through Red Dove, but the nun only brushed past the door, squeezing her tighter against the wall.

"Well now," Sister Agatha sniffed, "to what do we owe this honor?"

"I wanted to know how the children were doing," said Jerusha, her voice sounding feeble.

"Settling in." Sister Agatha lowered herself into the stiff-backed chair at the opposite end of the table, reached for her glasses and picked up a piece of paper.

"How does she seem… the girl, I mean?" Jerusha tilted her birdlike head and went on. "She's especially clever, you know—"

"She has much to learn." Sister Agatha squinted at the document she was holding and pushed it back down again. "You've done the right thing, bringin' 'em here."

"I certainly hope so. Red Dove—Mary, that is—shows a lot of promise. She speaks English, talks in full sentences—"

"Does she now? Then she knows more than she lets on. Indians often do. They like to deceive."

That's not true!

"Maybe you're right," said Jerusha. "All I know is, when she starts to speak, she puts her hand to her throat like this." Jerusha patted her neck. "I wonder if it's some sort of Native practice."

Sister Agatha arched an eyebrow. "Touchin' an amulet, prob'ly. Nasty habit. We'll soon break her of it."

Oh no you won't! thought Red Dove, as she watched the nun's fingers fiddle with the beads that dangled from her waist.

"But I am surprised to see you back so soon... Miss Kincaide, is it? Was it something you were forgetting or are we to expect your presence every day? We're very busy."

"I just came to see how my charges were doing. I'm a busy woman too—"

"You can't see the children now. They won't learn anythin' if you won't leave 'em alone."

"But I brought them."

"And you'll be glad you did. It's what you wanted, isn't it, to see they're raised proper?"

"Yes—" Jerusha faltered, looking confused.

Don't give up now! Red Dove wanted to cry out, sensing that if Jerusha did, there would be no going back to the life she knew. She searched the nun's face. It was blank, impassive, the pupils in her eyes tiny pinpricks surrounded by watery blue. She was about to step out from behind the door, anything to prevent being given away to this horrible creature in the black robe. And then she heard Jerusha's words.

"You're right. One day we'll all be grateful that we've taken this step," said Jerusha, sounding defeated.

"So if you'll excuse me."

"But we haven't talked about the boy—"

"We've said all we need," said Sister Agatha. "I have work to do." She nodded at the door.

Jerusha saw she was being dismissed. She rose awkwardly. "I am a teacher you know, so maybe—"

"Yes. Thank you." Sister Agatha's tight smile meant the discussion was at an end. "And you can come out of there now, Mary," she added, as her smile melted.

Red Dove's blood froze in her veins. She stepped from behind the door.

"Have you been here all along, my dear?" Jerusha, startled, rose from her chair and rushed over to Red Dove.

"Yes."

"Well… then… you're going to be fine. Isn't she, Sister?"

"Take us with you," Red Dove blurted, looking straight at Sister Agatha. "Get us out of here."

"Oh, my dear, I can't. I'm not responsible. That's what you said, isn't it, Sister?"

"'Tis."

Jerusha's eyebrows came together with concern. "Shouldn't you go and join the others? I think I saw them in the chapel." She reached out to touch a strand of hair that had fallen across her forehead.

"Take me with you," Red Dove tried once more.

But Jerusha didn't answer. Instead, she dropped her hand when she saw Sister Gertrude plodding towards them.

"*Komm*, Mary," Sister Gertrude said, breathing heavily and grabbing Red Dove's arm. "Time to cut your hair."

"No!" Red Dove pulled away.

"Oh dear," Jerusha soothed. She lifted one of Red Dove's glossy black braids. "It's a pity to lose your lovely hair, but I'm sure it will turn out all right. She let the braid drop. "And now," she sighed, "it's time for me to go, since you're no longer my responsibility."

"That's right," said Sister Agatha.

That's *not* right, Red Dove wanted to shout. You brought us here, so we *are* your responsibility.

>> Haircut <<

"Hurry up, Mary. Zat's vat zey call you, *nein?*" Sister Gertrude lumbered across the floor and dragged a three-legged stool to the center of the kitchen. She mopped her greasy forehead with a damp rag. "How old are you? Tvelf maybe? You haf gray eyes. You part vite?"

Red Dove approached slowly, unsure of what was happening. She didn't understand what she was supposed to do with the round wooden object that stood small, squat and ugly before her.

"Sit," ordered the nun.

"You shtink." Sister Gertrude pinched her nose.

Red Dove *did* smell, but it wasn't her fault. She hadn't washed in days, hadn't been near a stream or a river, or even a pot of clean water. She bent her head, ashamed.

"Here," said the nun, pointing at the rag swimming in a bucket of evil-smelling brown liquid. She set the bucket next to a tub of dark, cloudy water. "Vash up *gut* or I do."

But she'll see the pouch—and take it away! Fingers tight around it, Red Dove bent over the bucket. The stench hit her nostrils.

"Kerosene," announced Sister Gertrude. "Kill anyzing you haf. Scrub *gut* so I can cut your hair."

Red Dove didn't move.

"*Böses Mädchen.* Bad girl." The nun pulled the dripping rag from the oily liquid and handed it to Red Dove. "Here. Vipe your face."

Red Dove touched it to her skin. It burned. "*Aaieee*," she cried and dropped the rag in the tub.

80

"*Dummkopf!* Zat vas clean vater, but I not change now."
The nun threw the rag back into the kerosene, sloshed it
round and rubbed it hard against Red Dove's cheek.

"I'll do it," Red Dove cried and grabbed the rag. She
dabbed at her tortured skin.

"*Na ja*, Mary," said the nun with a grim smile. "Take off
your dress and vash mit kerosene und zen mit vater. Or I call
Sister Agatha." The nun's eyes glinted as she lowered herself
onto a chair. "*Und* you don't vant *zat*."

"Sister Agatha's callin' for ya," said a young nun, peering
in through the doorway.

"*Gott in Himmel.*" Sister Gertrude raised herself off the
chair and waddled to the door. Then she looked back at Red
Dove. "*Verstehst du?* I come back."

Red Dove crept to the door and closed it carefully. She
stared at the grimy bucket, the pasty yellow wall, the blackened
stovepipe that snaked across the ceiling. Tears blurred her
vision as she fumbled with her dress. Picking up the vile-
smelling rag, she began to rub the sharp, poisonous liquid into
her skin.

"Finish?" Sister Gertrude asked, plodding back into the
room.

Red Dove turned away and struggled to pull on her dress.
"Yes," she murmured, fingers on the pouch hidden just below
her collar.

"Now hair."

Sister Gertrude opened the brass-hinged door of a wooden
cabinet that hung from the wall. She reached in and pulled
out a pair of gleaming metal blades tipped with silvery rings.

Red Dove lunged from the stool, but Sister Gertrude was

quicker. She grabbed Red Dove's arm, wrenched it behind her and jerked her down. "Scissors, you shtupid girl!" she yelled.

Red Dove, powerless against the mountain of flesh that was Sister Gertrude, gave in.

"*Besser*," the nun soothed when she saw Red Dove was not going to resist. Sister Gertrude grabbed her braid and Red Dove, rigid now, stared straight ahead.

Why is she cutting my hair? We only do that when someone dies. *Did* someone die? Is it... *Walks Alone?*

Fighting panic, she began to count silently in her language, *wanji, numpa, yamni...* to block the terrifying images that filled her thoughts. She felt metal, heard the strange *slinch slinch slinch* as the blades sliced through her hair. Suddenly one side of her head felt light.

"No," she cried and leapt off the stool. A slap hit her full in the face and the scissors clattered to the floor.

She struggled to stay upright. Through a blur of pain, she saw the devastation. There before her was the hair she had tended since infancy, the hair she would cut only to honor the death of a loved one.

Red Dove felt for the other braid that still clung to her head.

You won't get this, she thought as her fingers curled around it. It's sacred. It holds memory. No one gave you permission to touch it—no one. She clenched her jaw and glared.

"You!" the nun sputtered, making the sign of the cross. "*Hexe*... vitch! Put spell on me, so I not stay. Somevun *else* finish." She picked up the shears. "But I take zese... in case."

>> My Name is Sister Mary Rose <<

Red Dove reached up and felt her butchered hair, the empty air where her braid had been. She was alone now, sitting on a stool in the kitchen, the reek of kerosene still clinging to her skin.

"What're ya doin', child?" called a voice behind her.

Red Dove bolted from the stool. "Who's there?"

"Didn't mean to startle ya." It was the young nun who had summoned Sister Gertrude. Her green eyes glowed under her feathery lashes, coal-black against the whiteness of her skin. "Sister Gertrude sent me to finish up." Crystal beads dangled from her waist and tinkled as she walked.

Red Dove put her hand to her throat, but all she felt was skin.

My pouch!

She looked down and saw it lying in the pile of hair on the floor, just as the broom the nun was wielding swept it up into the shovel.

"Don't," she cried. "It's mine!"

"What? It's just a pile of old hair."

Red Dove raced over, picked it out and closed her fist tight around the soft little bundle. "It's *Wakan*... sacred... magic," she stammered.

"Your hair's magic? Well, keep some of it then, if ya like, but let me clean the rest up or I'll be in for an encounter with Sister Agatha. And I don't want to get in trouble again." The nun went back to her sweeping.

She didn't see the pouch, Red Dove thought as the nun made circles around her.

And then Red Dove realized something else.

I understood every word she was saying, even words I never heard before, like "encounter"—but I knew what she meant... and I wasn't touching the pouch!

The nun stopped sweeping and looked at Red Dove. "Somethin' wrong, child?"

"No."

"Then let's just have another go with them scissors, shall we? Ya look right funny with only one braid."

Red Dove pulled away.

"Come now. I'm not gonna hurt ya. I just want to fix ya up a bit. We can't leave your hair like that. Here. Look at yourself." She pulled a gleaming silver disc from the pocket of her robe.

Red Dove stared into the glass. "Is that... me?"

"Haven't ya ever seen a mirror before, silly?" The nun tilted the disc so that Red Dove could see her tear-stained eyes, butchered hair and all. "We're not s'posed to have 'em— makes us vain, Sister Agatha says—so don't ya go tellin' on me now." She shoved the mirror back in her pocket. "Come on. Let me even it out a bit. You'll look ever so much prettier."

Red Dove bit her lip. She's right. I can't leave my hair like this.

"Good then," said the nun. She pulled something else out of her pocket and Red Dove gasped.

"It's just a brush, silly. I'm not gonna hurt ya." She rubbed the bristles against her open palm and smiled. "See? It's me own. Soft boar bristles." She reached out and patted Red Dove's hair with her gentle fingers. "There now. Nothin' to worry about. My name is Sister Mary Rose," she said, touching the brush gently to Red Dove's hair, "an' I'm a lot like you, ya know—"

"You're one of my people?"

"Course not," the young nun laughed. "I'm from the old country, Ireland. But I had to leave my home, like you, an' learn strange new ways. An' I'm *still* learnin', so maybe we can do some of that together. Would ya like that?"

Yes, thought Red Dove, nodding slowly.

"We have magic too, you know, where I come from."

"What kind of magic?"

"Oh, many kinds. And one day maybe I'll show you. But now... hold still." Sister Mary Rose reached into her pocket again. "They're sewin' shears, but they'll have to do."

Slinch, slinch, slinch they went. Red Dove closed her eyes and gritted her teeth, but this time the sound was accompanied by the high light melody the nun was humming. It was oddly reassuring.

And when the nun had finished, she pulled out the mirror and held it up so Red Dove could see.

The cut was even now, in line with Red Dove's chin. She tried to smile, but couldn't.

I *am* in mourning, she thought, for the life I used to live, for the people I loved.

"They cut my hair too when I became a nun," said Sister Mary Rose. "Shorter'n that. Practically shaved it all off. But I got used to it. You will too. Less bother. You might even come to like it one day."

Never! thought Red Dove, staring at the lonely little braid that lay with the sweepings on the floor.

The Frost Moon

Mission Boarding School

The Reservation—Late Fall, 1890

≫ Where'd Ya Learn that Tune? ≪

Summer gave way to fall, and the sweet smell of bonfires mingled with mist that rose from the leaf-covered ground. Months had passed since Red Dove came to the school. She longed to be outside in the crisp fall air. Looking through the open window, she saw boys in the fields, chopping wood and hauling logs for the fire.

Is Walks Alone with them? she wondered, as her thoughts were more and more with her family. Red Dove tried not to worry, but doing the tasks she was given—up to her elbows in a suds-filled sink, or standing at an ironing board for hours— left her too much time to think.

We're not learning anything here, she thought, as she watched the other girls in the steamy, crowded laundry. They say we're learning "gainful employment," but we're just doing jobs white people won't. She pulled another damp sheet from the never-empty basket at her feet and began to hum.

"Where'd ya learn that tune, child?" said Sister Mary Rose, coming up behind her.

"From you, Sister. Isn't it what you were singing when you cut my hair?"

"Why bless my soul, what a good ear ya have! But be careful singin' it around here." The nun's eyes gleamed. "It's about magic. Spirits ya know—"

"Spirits?" Red Dove's ears perked up.

"'Tis. *Banshees* and *lenanshees*—the kind we have in Ireland... and a certain person don't want us talkin' about 'em—says it goes against the teachin' of the Church."

"But *you* were singing it," Red Dove said.

"That I was."

"So you're not afraid—"

"Course not," said Sister Mary Rose. Then she walked over and shut the door tight. "Just a precaution." She marched up to the front of the crowded room. "Girls," she said, arching an eyebrow, "I don't know why we shouldn't be able to enjoy a song now and then, do you?"

Thirty pairs of eyes looked up from their tasks.

"So go ahead, Mary."

"What?" Red Dove asked.

"Give us a song."

"Here? Now?"

Sister Mary Rose nodded. "Wasn't that what you were

doin' a moment ago? Now you have an audience—"

. Red Dove looked around. The other girls were watching her, curious, waiting to see what would happen. She saw Miriam smirk. Red Dove raised her head and opened her mouth, but nothing came out. The sound stuck somewhere between her throat and belly.

"Ya can do it. I know ya can." The nun's dark eyebrows rose high with encouragement.

Someone snickered.

Red Dove took a breath, opened her mouth and this time a squeak emerged.

Miriam giggled.

"That's enough, Miriam," warned Sister Mary Rose.

Red Dove took another breath, deeper now, and the squeak became a steady thrum that filled her chest, surged up and flowed from her mouth. Full-throated, and sharing Sister's strange, intoxicating tune, she rode the sound until the song came to its mournful, satisfying end.

She stopped and looked around. Hannah's round, dark eyes stared up in rapt attention. The others watched with strange expressions.

What just happened?

Sister Mary Rose clapped her hands and broke the spell. "Lovely," she exclaimed.

The rush of applause was abrupt, startling, and oddly welcome. And when it finished, Red Dove ducked her head, embarrassed, and yet somehow pleased.

"Thank you, Mary. Now shall I tell ya what the song is about, since ya didn't know the words." Sister Mary Rose again squinted at the door to see that it was closed. "It's one from me country, about spirits, like I said—but I don't know if ya have 'em here. I'm talkin' about a mischievous fairy, who puts a spell on a poor, unsuspectin' young girl, to make 'er fall in love with a cruel man—an' get 'erself in trouble—" Sister Mary Rose went on. "The world is full of spirits, just waitin' to put spells on people an' break their hearts. But don't let anyone know that we been talkin' 'bout magic—"

"Why?" asked Hannah.

"Because Sister Agatha doesn't put much faith in fairies, or magic, an' you could get me in real trouble if she found out," said the nun, searching the faces around.

"Oh, we would *never* tell, Sister," said Miriam with a catlike grin. "Promise."

›› We'll Summon the Spirits ‹‹

"Sister Agatha left ya here to finish up by yourself again, didn't she? I don't know why she works ya so hard." Sister Mary Rose looked around the laundry, empty now but for the two of them. "She seems to have it in for ya."

"She does," said Red Dove, as she dragged the last damp sheet from the basket and draped it over the ironing board, too tired to say more.

"Well, tomorrow is her day to go to town for supplies, an' she'll be leavin' Sister Gertrude in charge, so I can make good on my promise—"

"What promise?"

"To show ya some of me magic, like I said. 'Less of course ya don't want that—"

"I do," said Red Dove, wondering what the nun had in store.

"Good then. I'll tell Sister Gertrude we're goin' to gather mushrooms—she loves mushrooms—so she'll let us go. Would ya like that, child?"

"Yes," said Red Dove, as her thoughts strayed to the smell of crisp fall air, the feel of earth beneath her feet, and the longed-for sight of open sky.

The next day dawned bright and clear, but by the time Sister Agatha left for town it was already afternoon. "Chust make sure she's varmly dressed," said Sister Gertrude. "Zere's too much sickness here *und* no medicine. Ve don't vant to lose anozzer vun. Sister Agatha has *Kopfschmerz.*" She pointed to her head. "So be back for vespers... or else."

The sun was high as they set off, but a moldy dampness still clung to the earth. Red Dove and Sister Mary Rose picked their way through piles of wet leaves and undergrowth.

The nun moved on ahead, her hand on a bulging leather satchel slung across her shoulder.

"What's in that?" Red Dove asked.

"Me magic, like I said."

Red Dove touched her fingers to the pouch and stared at the nun's back, trying to see what she was thinking, but all she learned was how happy she was to be out on a bright fall day.

As they emerged from the shelter of the trees, Red Dove saw a patch of earth, surrounded by a circle of sparse, yellow grass. Inside the circle, the earth was hard and bare.

"An old Indian camp, most like," said Sister. "See there— ashes from an ancient fire. A perfect place for magic... as promised." Her eyes crinkled into a smile as she lowered herself onto a log and patted the space beside her. "Come. Sit."

The nun reached into the satchel and pulled out a round, flat object, painted green and covered with a tightly stretched animal skin. "D'ya know what this is?" she asked.

"Of course. A drum," said Red Dove.

"Not just any drum, silly. It's a *bodhran*, an *Irish* drum. And not just any *bodhran*. It was me grandmother's. If you play it right, you'll call up the spirits. An' their magic." She beamed.

"I never saw it before—"

"I keep it hidden. Sister Agatha hates singin' an' dancin', an' she's always mad at me anyway... so she doesn't have to know 'bout this now, does she?" Sister Mary Rose reached back into the satchel, pulled out a small wooden stick and began tapping a steady rhythm, a rollicking, repetitive *tatatata*.

Red Dove felt her body begin to sway. She watched her feet rise and fall and rise and fall again, pounding a pattern on the earth.

"Take 'em off," said the nun.

"What?" said Red Dove.

"Your boots. They're hurtin' ya, I can tell."

Red Dove pulled at the stiff leather and tore the boots from her feet. She felt the cool, moist earth against her skin.

"Better, no?" said Sister.

"Yes," murmured Red Dove, lost to the rhythm of the drum.

"So we'll summon the spirits, jus' the two of us together, and there'll be nary a soul to stop us," Sister cried as she finished one song and started another.

≫ Late ≪

They danced and sang for what seemed just a moment, but when Red Dove looked up, the sun was on the horizon.

"Oh no!" she cried. "Sister Gertrude said to be back by vespers, and now it's that time at least."

Sister Mary Rose stopped drumming. "What?" She squinted through unfocused eyes.

"It's late—"

"Jesus, Mary and Joseph! Sister Agatha'll have me hide for sure. Why didn't ya stop me then?"

"I thought you were paying attention—"

"An' I thought *you* were." Sister Mary Rose shoved the drum inside the satchel. "We're in for it," she said with a wildness in her eye.

"What will she do?"

"Nothin' good, I can tell ya."

"Can't you use your magic?"

"That *was* me magic," said the nun with a shrug.

"That?"

"Why sure. The dancin', the drummin'—"

"*All* of it?"

"'Twas. Didn't it make ya feel better?"

"Yes, but… I didn't see any spirits. They didn't come."

"How d'ya know?" The nun shrugged and hoisted the satchel onto her shoulder.

Red Dove decided not to argue. "But what are we going to do about Sister Agatha?" she asked instead.

"What would you like me to do, child—turn her into a nicer person?"

"I just thought—"

"Stop thinkin' an' start gatherin' mushrooms. Fast as ya can, so we've somethin' to show." She started heading back towards the woods. Red Dove watched her scan the damp soil around the roots and close her fingers around a tiny yellow fungus.

"Not that—it's poison!" Red Dove shouted.

Startled, the nun dropped the little mushroom.

"Better let me," said Red Dove. "My grandfather showed me how—"

"Yes, yes," muttered the nun, as distracted, her fingers closed around a bright purple flower. "You pick the mushrooms and I'll gather herbs while I'm here. Sister Agatha won't believe we've spent all this time just lookin' for mushrooms. And she's been in a terrible mood lately—"

"With her headaches," Red Dove said.

"How'd you know she had headaches?" Sister Mary Rose said, stopping to look up.

"I just knew... from looking at her face—"

"What nonsense are ya talkin'? How can lookin' at her face tell ya anythin'?"

"I can read people's thoughts," blurted Red Dove.

"Oh go on with ya." Sister Mary Rose gave a dismissive wave.

"It's true. I can."

"You're a mind-reader?" Sister Mary Rose laughed. She threw the grass and flowers she was holding into her satchel and straightened. "Why don't ya read mine then? Go on. Tell me what I'm thinkin'."

Red Dove touched her fingers to the pouch. "You're thinking... that you don't believe me. About being able to read people's thoughts—"

"Course. Anyone could know that. But what else? What am I thinkin' 'bout now... exactly."

"You're thinking... about... Sister Agatha—"

"But what am I thinkin' *about* her?" Sister Mary Rose sighed.

Red Dove watched the nun's face and waited. And the words fell out of her mouth. "You're wondering why she's so cold. And mean. You're wondering what she was like when she was young."

Sister Mary Rose tilted her head and narrowed her eyes. "Go on."

"When she was Ma... Ma... "

"Holy Mother o' God. How'd ya know her name was Maura?" The young nun's eyes widened with shock.

I guessed, thought Red Dove—or did I know, because of the pouch? And remembered her grandfather's warning not to talk about it. "Was that what Sister Agatha was called before she became a nun... Maura?"

"How could ya possibly know? Only a few people do." Sister Mary Rose looked straight at Red Dove and tilted her head. "So ya must be tellin' the truth—you really are a mind reader." Sister Mary Rose put a finger to her cheek. "So maybe we can put it to good use."

"How?"

"You tell me, *if* ya know what I'm thinkin' that is—what should we do?"

Red Dove, fingers to the pouch, watched the nun's face. "You're thinking that if *I* know what's in Sister Agatha's mind, then I can give her an excuse that she'll believe—"

"My thoughts exactly," laughed the nun.

>> What Just Happened? <<

The door burst open as Red Dove and Sister Mary Rose raced up to the school. Sister Agatha stood glaring, lips compressed, eyes angry slits beneath her brow. "Where have you been, Sister?" she hissed.

Red Dove looked at Sister Mary Rose, waiting for her to answer. She didn't.

"Well?"

"Sister Gertrude sent us for mushrooms," Red Dove blurted.

"Mushrooms? Stupid woman," Sister Agatha roared. "Mushrooms're poison. She'll eat herself into her grave. And why were you gone so long?"

Red Dove touched her pouch and searched the nun's face. "We wanted to find something… for your headaches."

"How did you know?" Sister Agatha put a hand to her forehead.

"We're sorry we took so long, but it was hard to find—"

"What was?"

"The plant you wanted," Red Dove blurted as the image of a flower with a bulging center surrounded by petals of bright purple came into her mind. "We have some, don't we?" she asked Sister Mary Rose and reached for the satchel. She pulled at the tangle of weeds and picked out the very one. "Is this it?" she said, holding it out.

"It is, exactly. Coneflower. Echinacea," said Sister Agatha, inspecting the plant, "but you're still late, so you'll do penance."

"Penance, penance, penance," Red Dove heard, as the voices around her began to fade, blending into a steady hum that filled

the room. Hand on the pouch, she heard a constant thump, thump, thump...

A heartbeat—is it mine or hers?

She felt dizzy, opened her mouth to take in air, and her head began to pound with a crushing pain.

A rush, a crash. Being lifted, carried up, exploded through a long tunnel... and out the other side.

What's happening?

She remembered what Sister Mary Rose had told her, all she knew about Sister Agatha... and understood: the heartbeat, the eyes she was seeing through, the thick black rage and ancient sorrow all belonged to someone else. They belonged to Sister Agatha. She was feeling what it was to be Sister Agatha... .

And suddenly, looking through another's eyes, and seeing, standing before her, not the angry old nun, but a dark-haired, copper-skinned girl with startling gray eyes.

I'm looking at myself—through her!

She tore her hand from her throat, jerked her head away and the vision stopped. Back in her own body now, she stared at the nun and swayed.

Sister Agatha put her hand to her forehead. "Strange," she muttered. "The pain was gone for just a moment." She straightened her spine and pursed her lips. "I'll use that coneflower," she said, "since you brought it. But you've missed your supper, Mary, and you'll have to do *all* the washin' up. I'll give you the rest of your punishment in the mornin'."

>> The Creature We Know Today <<

"Why didn't you say anything?" asked Red Dove when at last she and Sister Mary Rose reached the safety of the kitchen.

"Guess I wasn't much help to ya, was I?" the young nun answered. "Maybe ya've noticed that Sister Agatha doesn't like me much—"

"She *hates* me."

"That she does." Sister Mary Rose reached out to brush a stray hair from Red Dove's cheek. "So maybe it's best we both stay out of her way for now—but I'll try to help ya as much as I can." She pulled an apron over her habit, wrapped the string around herself and tied it in front. "But ya did seem to know just what to say to her. Could ya really tell what she was thinkin'?"

"Yes," Red Dove said slowly, wondering how much of the sudden knowledge was due to the pouch. "But something else happened. I saw myself."

Sister Mary Rose picked up a plate, shoved it in the soapy water and frowned. "What d'ya mean?"

"As she did, through *her* eyes, like I was inside her, looking out—"

"Holy Mother o' God!" Sister Mary Rose crossed herself rapidly.

"It's true. I *felt* her rage towards me—and some pain she remembered—"

"No surprise, there," exclaimed Sister Mary Rose with a brittle laugh. "She's got a lot to be tormented about, if what they say is true—"

"What? Tell me."

"Och." Sister Mary Rose shrugged. "Just stories, maybe, 'bout a man who betrayed her back in Ireland. An' broke 'er heart."

"Sister Agatha has a heart?"

"Hard to believe, isn't it? That she could be in love?" Sister Mary Rose giggled. "She was pretty back then, they say." Her eyes gleamed wickedly. "The man, an Irish soldier, promised to marry her—but he did not. He left Ireland to come here an' make his fortune. Abandoned her. And then, well... ." Her cheeks flushed pink, she lowered her voice and put her hand in front of her mouth. "She learned she was carryin' his child," she whispered. "D'ya understand?"

"I know what happens between men and women," Red Dove said, remembering what her mother had told her—the things every girl should know.

"Good, then I don't need to explain. Havin' a baby out o' wedlock is a grievous sin, ya know, and Sister Agatha's family disowned her when they found out. She went to the only place she could—a convent—"

"And she became a nun?"

"She did... after she had her baby—"

"Was it a girl?"

"How'd ya know?" said Sister Mary Rose, pursing her lips. "Och, go on with ya. Stop readin' me mind, will ya!"

"I'm not." Red Dove's hands were busy in the soapy water and she wasn't touching the pouch. "I was just guessing—"

"Well stop it, would ya? Yes, the baby was a girl, they tell me, but she died, poor thing."

"How awful for her—"

"You feel pity for that woman?" Sister Mary Rose pulled her own soapy hands from the water and wiped them on her apron. "Wish I could. Maybe it *did* break her heart, but it hardened her as well and she became the creature we know today as—"

"Sister Agatha!" they both said, laughing grimly.

"Anyways, years later she came to this country, determined to find the child's father. Maybe she still loved him. She heard he'd become a soldier, posted near here. And *then* she found out he'd married an Indian woman, an' had a child by *her*—"

"One of my people?"

Sister Mary Rose shrugged. "Dunno. Happens all the time. But when Sister Agatha found out, it nearly did her in." Her face darkened. "She *hates* Indians more'n anythin'."

"Maybe this is her way of getting even—"

"Maybe." Sister Mary Rose narrowed her eyes at Red Dove. "Ya feelin' all right, child? Ya seem a little peaked." She touched Red Dove's forehead. "Hmmm," she said, and walked over to the small wooden bench by the window, reached for the satchel and began pulling out bits of greenery. "Ya might need some of them herbs yourself. Here's what I found. Sage for cookin', an' some others too: yarrow to soothe, rosemary to calm, and this… 'specially for you." She pulled out a purple blossom and crushed it between her thumb and forefinger.

"I know that plant. It's windflower—"

"Do ya now? I was readin' about it. Said it'd do ya good."

"Yes it will, but only if it's dried. It'll make you sick if—"

The nun didn't hear. "It'll make ya forget your homesickness, the book said."

Red Dove nodded. "Grandfather used to make tea from it. He drank some the day my grandmother died, I remember. To ease the pain of loss." But she remembered something else he'd told her as well: that the flower was powerful medicine— but only when dried. "If you drink it when it's fresh it will make you sick."

"Nonsense," said Sister Mary Rose, picking up a wilted blossom. "It's the same flower isn't it, fresh or dried? Anyway, I'm sure this is dry enough. We picked it hours ago."

"Yes, but—"

"Sister Agatha vant you!" Sister Gertrude poked her head in the door. She pointed at Sister Mary Rose.

"What now?" She turned back to Red Dove. "I guess I have to leave ya to it, then, but I'll be back—and in the meantime, don't forget to brew yourself some tea."

>> Windflower Tea <<

Hours passed.

I'll be up all night, Red Dove thought as she stared at the mountain of pans still teetering in the sink. And where is Sister Mary Rose? She said she'd be back to help. She looked at the pile of herbs and flowers the nun had left. Maybe the tea *will* make me feel better… is it dry enough yet?

She boiled some water, poured it in a clean mug, grabbed a handful of the wilted windflower blossoms, and dropped them in. Then she touched her lips to the rim.

Hot!

She walked over to the window, put the cup on the sill to cool and stared out through the wavy glass. Exhausted as she was, she let her thoughts wander to the events of the day.

For a moment, I knew what it was like to be Sister Agatha… but I don't *want* to. She's mad at the world, and she's taking her anger out on everyone, especially me.

Sister Gertrude appeared in the open doorway again. "Sister Agatha vant a cup of tea. Coneflower. For her head. Now," she barked.

"All right." Red Dove watched the nun stomp away and had a thought. Windflower eases the pain of loss and Sister Agatha might need that more than I do… so if she drinks it, maybe she won't be so angry.

Red Dove pulled a handful of coneflowers, and dropped them into the still steaming mug. Gathering her courage, she crossed the floor of the kitchen, walked down the long corridor to Sister Agatha's room, and knocked.

There was no response, so she tried again. Finally, she heard a growl from inside. "Come in," it said.

Red Dove opened the door and stepped in.

"Close the door."

Red Dove did. She heard a dull *clack, clack* from the rosary beads swinging from a hook on the wall beside it. The shades were drawn and the light was dim. As her eyes adjusted, she could just make out a blurry shape by the window. "Well, what do you want?" it said.

"I … brought you some tea, Sister."

"Coneflower? Put it on the table."

"It's coneflower, and other herbs… to make you feel better."

"Other herbs? Why?" Sister Agatha crossed the floor, dark robes swishing, blacker than the blackness.

Suddenly, Red Dove saw her: her fleshy white head was exposed, naked—bald.

"What other herbs?" the nun barked.

"Herbs so you won't be sad and angry," Red Dove blurted. "Windflower."

"Are you mad? Windflower's poison!" the nun shrieked. "Everyone knows that!"

"Not if it's dry… Sister Mary Rose thought—"

The slap came down. The mug crashed to the floor. Burning liquid splashed Red Dove's hand and spewed across the room. She lurched for the door, turned the handle and ran.

"She tried to poison me! Stop her!"

Red Dove burst into the kitchen, looked wildly around and scurried under the oilcloth that covered the table. She listened to the hubbub that followed, the startled nuns and shrieks from Sister Agatha.

I can't hide here forever, she thought, staring at the yellow plaster walls, watching a spider crawl slowly down its web towards a doomed, struggling fly. I trusted Sister Mary Rose, but she was wrong. What can I trust? She closed her fingers tight around the pouch, desperate for the comfort of its soothing drone. "Tell me," she whispered, and as the waiting wore on, the flagstones felt even harder, colder. Finally, she let out a shuddering sigh and dropped her hand.

It's the pouch's fault, she decided at last. It tells me things I don't want to hear, makes me feel things I don't want to feel, makes me know what it is to *be* Sister Agatha—when I don't want to. Maybe… Grandfather was wrong. Maybe… the pouch is cursed.

And if I keep using it, I will be too, she thought, pulling the little amulet from her neck and stuffing it inside her pocket.

≫ We Do Not Hate ≪

"Been here ze whole night, haf you?" Sister Gertrude's great bug eyes peered at Red Dove from underneath the lifted oilcloth. "Get in line mit ze others und Sister Agatha vill deal mit you later," she mumbled, heaving her heavy body up off the floor.

Red Dove crept slowly out from under the table, straightened and walked down the hall. Moving quietly, she ambled up behind the other girls and joined the end of the line, heading for chapel. She didn't want to attract attention, but no one seemed to notice. And no one spoke to her. Am I invisible? she wondered, and reached for the pouch for the answer. Then dropped her hand. No, I won't use it anymore. It's got me in enough trouble already.

The day wore on and still no one paid any attention to her, until at last she dragged herself to the class she dreaded most, the one with Sister Agatha.

"Sit there," said the nun, pointing to a desk at the back of the room "so I don't have to look at your ugly face." She turned and wrote something on the board.

Sister Gertrude poked her head through the doorway. "Somevun to see you, Sister," she called. "Vaiting in your office."

"Whatever could it be now?" Sister Agatha put down the chalk. "Remain exactly as you are, children. *Especially* you, Mary. Don't you dare move."

Dizzy from lack of sleep, Red Dove waited, struggling to stay upright in her seat behind the rest of the class. No one can see me, she thought, with their backs all turned. I'll put my head down for a moment.

The hard wood was cool against her cheek. She closed her eyes. The room, quiet at first, filled with small noises. Random whispers became a steady drone. She was tempted to reach for the pouch, now hidden deep within her pocket, but decided against it.

I don't want to know what they're thinking, so I won't try

to use it, or even look at their faces, or listen. All I want to do is sleep.

A tang of burning sage.

A voice: "Gray Eyes."

Grandfather! I'm not using the pouch.

"You should. It will help you understand others—"

I don't want to! I don't care what people are thinking or feeling—not if they're people I hate.

"We do not hate, Gray Eyes—"

Don't make me use it, Grandfather. It's nothing but trouble.

"With it, you will find your power—"

I don't have any power.

"You do. So watch. And listen."

The smell of burning sage growing stronger. Smoke filling the air. Grandfather's kindly old face coming into view. "This is something that happened long ago."

But I don't want to see it—

"Do as I ask."

A rumble, a sound of galloping hooves from far away. An image forming and the outline of a man carrying a lance and painted for battle.

"Crazy Horse. The leader of our people—"

The one who defeated Custer?

"Yes."

The man, surrounded by a band of warriors, approaching a white man's fort.

"He is there to ask for peace."

The sun crossing the courtyard as white soldiers march in. A warrior walking up to Crazy Horse, taking him by the hand and leading him past the lines of men and guns to one of the buildings.

Why are there bars on the windows?

"He's taking him to jail—"

Who would do that?

"Little Big Man. Crazy Horse's friend—"

He can't be his friend, if he's taking him to jail!

"Crazy Horse was warned that he would be invincible in battle, that bullets and guns would never touch him, but that his end would come at the hand of a friend."

Can't we stop him?

"This has already happened."

Gazing in horror as Little Big Man pushes Crazy Horse towards the prison. Crazy Horse drawing his knife, slashing Little Big Man's arm to the bone and wrenching himself free.

A soldier carrying a bayonet with a blade the length of an arm, stabbing Crazy Horse in the back, pushing his body deep onto the blade, and tearing his flesh.

He's killing him, Grandfather! Why won't anyone stop him?

"They hated him—"

His people?

"They were afraid, some of them and ashamed—because he was not."

And this is how they paid him for being brave? Were they sorry afterwards?

"When it was too late. Some of his people joined Sitting Bull in Grandmother's Land, a place they call Canada, where they were cold and hungrier still. They came back to the reservation when the Government promised them food and shelter—"

And did they get it?

"Promises were broken and the people starved—"

Like the ones I saw begging for food, that day at the fort... but our family didn't stay on the reservation. Why?

"Because your white father bargained with the soldiers so we were not forced to go—"

Then he did try to help—but he broke his promises too and left us hungry. I know I shouldn't hate, Grandfather, but sometimes I can't help it—

"We do not hate, Gray Eyes... ," repeated the voice, more softly now. "The past cannot be changed, but the future can—"

Then tell me how! Red Dove wanted to yell as she felt the onslaught of tears.

"The pouch," was all it said.

>> Everything's Backwards <<

"Wake up, Mary" First came the shout and then the slap.

Red Dove pulled her hand to her stinging mouth. She looked up at the nun and the faces in the room. She saw the gleam in Miriam's eye.

Sister Agatha clicked her rosary beads. "You're the laziest girl in the class, sleeping through the lesson. You can't do anything right."

"Sister?" she heard.

"What, Miriam?"

"She *can* do things. She sang us a song about spirits, like the ones native people believe in." Miriam paused and looked at Red Dove. "Like saints and angels, Sister Mary Rose said—"

"Sister Mary Rose? Is that what she's teaching you?" Sister Agatha's nostrils flared. "That heathen ideas are the same as the teachings of the Church?"

The girls looked at each other frantically, but no one responded. They knew what was coming.

"It's because of you, isn't it?" Sister Agatha said to Red Dove. "Songs about spirits, heathen teachings? Come up here, Mary. Let's see what you learned… while you were asleep."

Miriam giggled.

"What year in history were we talking about? Write it on the board."

Red Dove's face burned, her throat ached and a dull pain moved from her chest to her throat as she walked to the front of the room.

Sister Agatha handed her a piece of chalk and she dragged it across the dusty black surface. *Scritch, scritch, scritch* it went, but her hand shook so much that the numbers were nothing but a scrawl.

"What's that supposed to be?" the nun barked. "Tell me."

"Fourteen ninety-two," Red Dove said weakly.

Miriam giggled again.

"'Fourteen ninety-two,'" the nun mocked in a high girlish voice. "And why is that date important?"

"Because that's when Columbus… ," Red Dove whispered.

"Speak up. I can't hear you," said the nun as she paced across the front of the room.

"It's when Columbus came to America—"

"It's when Columbus *discovered* America—"

"He didn't—"

"He *didn't?*" Sister Agatha stopped abruptly.

"Our people were here already—"

Another slap hit Red Dove full in the face and the room began to spin.

"Stupid girl. How dare you? Write it down, now, a hundred times all over the board. Fourteen ninety-two, the year Columbus discovered America."

Red Dove's hands were shaking so much she could barely hold the chalk. She looked at the board, but the lines began to blur, and suddenly everything seemed wrong. "It's all backwards—"

"Backwards? I'll give you backwards," screamed the nun, grabbing a fistful of hair. "How dare you question my authority… and try to poison me!"

"*Poison, poison, poison*," roared in Red Dove's ears as her legs buckled and she fell to the floor.

Wanichokan Wi

The Winter Moon

Mission Boarding School
The Reservation—Winter, 1890

>> A Celtic Cross <<

Days passed in a haze of fever, and when Red Dove opened her eyes at last, it was evening, and the pale gray walls and cold metal beds of the empty sick room only deepened the gloom.

She could see through the snow-covered window to the hill beyond. There, in the ashy dusk, was a small but growing clump of crosses below the windmill on the crest.

Where other girls are buried, she thought, girls like me... .

"Back with us at last, are ya," came a cheerful, chirping voice, breaking into her thoughts. Sister Mary Rose hovered over her, straightening covers and fluffing her pillow. "Better now?"

"How long have I been here?" Red Dove asked.

"No more'n a few days."

"*Days?* What happened?"

"Can't tell ya much, 'cause I don't know meself. Sister Agatha locked me in me room—for tryin' to poison her, she said."

"But you didn't—"

"Course not. It was you who gave it to her—"

"You said the herb was dry enough—"

"Och, child, why would ya listen to a poor Irish girl like me? What would I know about the plants round here? I've no head for matters like that."

"But you said—"

"An' I'm truly sorry. D'ya forgive me?" said the nun, leaning in close.

Red Dove nodded. "I do. But what if I *had* drunk it—"

"Then I'd never be able to forgive meself... but what if she had? Now there's a thought," Sister Mary Rose said with a twinkle in her eye. "That kinda accident might'a solved a lot o' problems." She smiled wickedly. "But come now. We're all glad you're better—least I am anyways. First I was afraid ya did drink the poison, but the doctor said no, and then we thought it might be consumption. That's what killed most o' them up there." Sister Mary Rose nodded at the cluster of graves, visible through the window. "But it was just influenza, thank the Lord, though bad enough to keep you here for days—"

"Did anyone come see me?" Red Dove asked, longing for word of her brother.

"Course. The doctor, Sister Gertrude, Miriam—"

"*Miriam?*"

"She was worried about ya, child. Everyone thought she was 'specially brave to come look after ya—"

"Look after me?"

"Sure. She could'a caught the fever herself, but she said no, she was goin' to be a Good Samaritan and take care o' ya—to be an example to the other girls. Not like her, is it?"

No, it's not, Red Dove thought, wondering what possible reason Miriam could have had for wanting to help.

Sister Mary Rose opened a small brown jar on the table near the bed, took a sniff and wrinkled her nose. "Camphor. Nasty stuff. I'll rub it on ya later," she said, and shoved the top back on. She plopped into the chair next to Red Dove's bed. "But now I want to show ya somethin' else." She reached into her pocket and pulled out a silver cross, with a ring in the center, encrusted with bits of green and amber glass and covered with strange markings. "Celtic. Me mother gave it to me before she died, when I was but a wee babe. She told the nuns who raised me that it would help find things that were lost."

"But why are you giving it to me?"

"I'm lettin' ya use it *because* it holds memories," the nun said impatiently. "I thought it might help ya find things—"

"What things?"

"Och, I don't know. People ya might be lookin' for... when ya need to, that is."

What is she talking about? Once again, Red Dove longed for the pouch to help her understand.

"I've never shown it to anyone here but you," Sister Mary

Rose went on. "Because *your* magic won't help ya find things, will it?"

"It brings me dreams and visions, and it helps me understand what people are thinking and feeling, so it might—"

"Well, try this anyway," the nun said, pushing the cross towards her.

"One bead's missing," Red Dove said.

"That it is. Been gone as long as I can remember."

Red Dove wrapped her fingers around it and felt the metal warm to her touch.

"Is it workin'?" the nun asked hopefully.

"I don't know," Red Dove said. "It's getting warmer." She held the object far from her body and the metal cooled. "No... it was probably just the heat of my body. Nothing seems to be happening."

"Nothin'?" asked the nun, disappointed. "It's not tellin' ya anythin' at all?"

"No," Red Dove said. "Maybe it doesn't really have any power—"

"How can ya say that?" A bright pink flush appeared on the nun's cheeks. "It was me mother's, I tell ya, an' it used to help *me* find things—"

"Used to?"

"Yes, but not much anymore. Maybe I'm too old. I thought you bein' so young an' all... but if you're so full of doubt, an' ya don't believe—"

"You're probably right, Sister," Red Dove said, handing the cross back to the nun and pulling the covers up to her chin. "It was probably meant for you alone." She saw the nun's expression. "I didn't mean to hurt your feelings." Red Dove turned her head and stared out the window at the snow-covered graves on the hill.

The nun caught her look. "Course ya didn't, child," she said, patting the covers. "You're just gettin' over bein' sick, an' you're worried. But everythin's goin' to be fine, I tell ya."

Red Dove watched her bustle around the room, sliding jars and bottles as she dusted the shelves, humming as she went. But there's something else she's not telling me. The minute the nun's back was turned, she reached over to the chair and felt the familiar lump inside the pocket of her dress. She shoved the pouch under the covers, and still holding it tight, listened for the familiar drone. At last she understood.

"It's Walks Alone, isn't it?" she blurted, sitting up straight, dread coursing through her.

Sister Mary Rose dropped her dust cloth. "You're readin' my thoughts again, aren't ya?" she sighed. "Well if ya must know, I brought ya the cross so you could tell us where to find him—"

"What do you mean?"

"He's run away. The priests were too hard on him, I think. They punished him for stealin'." Sister Mary Rose rushed over to the bed and pushed Red Dove gently back down on the pillow. "Don't go gettin' alarmed—"

"What did he steal?"

"Sister Agatha's diary, they said—"

"He wouldn't."

"Try tellin' that to Sister Agatha. He heard you were sick, rushed into her office an' demanded to see ya. She wouldn't let him, of course, so the priests had to haul him off." Sister Mary

Rose tilted her head and leveled her cool green eyes at Red Dove. "After he left, she noticed her diary went missin'. Ya never heard a woman scream an' yell so much. Makes ya want to know what was in it, no?" she said with a wink.

But Red Dove didn't share her glee. "What happened to him?" she asked, holding her breath as she waited for the answer.

"Beat him, if ya must know." The nun looked nervously at Red Dove. "Then locked him in a closet. He got out somehow, and run away—"

"I have to find him." Red Dove dropped her feet to the floor.

Sister Mary Rose shoved her back down onto the bed. "Ya can't. You're too weak. Just lie still an' get better." Sister Mary Rose gave her another firm push. "He's goin' to be fine, I tell ya. If ya get some sleep, things'll look a whole lot brighter in the mornin'. An' if you're not wantin' this," she said, holding up the cross, "I'll be takin' it back."

"I won't be going anywhere... tonight," she whispered after the nun had left the room. "But can I trust you?"

>> Red-Handed <<

The hours hung heavy as Red Dove waited for dawn. She longed for sleep, but was too afraid. At last, a milky glow seeped through the little window. She listened hard, but apart from a few scattered rustlings, all was quiet. She pulled off the covers and lowered her feet to the frigid floor. The morning chill froze her breath as she wrapped a blanket around her shoulders and, reaching under the mattress, stuffed the pouch carefully between the thin pad and the metal bedframe.

Pushing aside the plain white curtain and gazing through the icy pane at the fields beyond, she scoured the horizon. There wasn't much to see—a dappled pony; trees, withered and lifeless against a leaden sky; squash and potatoes harvested; corn stalks cut; hay mowed.

Where is he? And how am I going to find him?

A sudden clatter from the kitchen told her the day had begun.

Too late now, she thought sadly, pulling the blanket tighter and climbing back into bed.

Sister Mary Rose burst into the room. "They're accusin' *you,* child. They're sayin' you took Sister Agatha's diary."

"I didn't!"

"I told 'em that, but Miriam said she saw ya with it—"

"She's lying."

"That she is, but they all think Walks Alone gave it to ya before he ran away, an' that you're hidin' it here, somewhere." Sister Mary Rose tilted her head. "So I said I'd come an' give a look. Let's prove 'em wrong, shall we?"

Red Dove nodded—and then realized: *If she does, she'll see the pouch.* "Don't."

"Why not? It's the only way." Before Red Dove could say more, the nun crouched down, curled her hand between the mattress and the bed frame, and jumped back. "Dear God," she gasped.

Did she find the pouch?

But it was something else the nun was holding: a small, red, velvet-covered book.

"What is it?" Red Dove asked.

"What d'ya think? Her diary. How d'ya explain it?"

"I didn't take it."

"An' I believe ya. 'Cause I have a pretty good idea who did—Miriam herself, most like. Hid it here whilst you were sleepin'." Sister Mary Rose opened the book and started scanning the pages. "That explains why she was so keen to look after ya—"

"We should give it back—"

"Do you know what Sister Agatha would do to ya if ya did?"

"Then we'd better hide it."

"Yes… just let me have a wee look first." The nun started riffling through the pages.

"Don't. You'll get us in *more* trouble. Hide it. Please," Red Dove begged, but Sister Mary Rose kept turning pages until she found something.

"Here, read this." She pushed the book under Red Dove's nose.

"I don't want to see it," Red Dove said.

"Then why'd you take it?" Sister Agatha roared, sweeping into the room and grabbing the diary. "Caught you both red-handed, didn't I?"

"I–" stammered Sister Mary Rose, too startled to say more.

"Reading my private diary," Sister Agatha thundered. "How *dare* you? Go and wait for me in my office," she said, nostrils flaring. "Now."

"Yes, Sister." Head down, Sister Mary Rose darted out of the room.

"And you. Come with me." Sister Agatha grabbed Red Dove by the collar of her nightgown and pulled her, barefoot and shivering, across the room, down the hall and into the chapel, accompanied by the steady *clack, clack, clack* of her wooden beads.

The other girls, sitting in their pews, stared as Red Dove was dragged to the front of the chapel. Her clothes were damp with sweat and her feet were cold against the hard stone floor.

Sister Agatha dropped her onto the foremost pew. "Sit there. Don't move."

Red Dove blinked and looked around. Pine boughs and Christmas ribbons covered the altar. Scents of beeswax and incense filled the air. She shivered.

"I have three announcements," said Sister Agatha, her cold eyes sweeping the room. "A boy has run away. George, a troublemaker. He made a foolish mistake, and if he's found, he'll see the error of his ways. And if he's not, well... that'll be the worse for him." She stared at the sea of frightened eyes. "He stole my diary." Her unblinking eyes bore down on Red Dove. "And gave it to his sister. Isn't that right, young lady?"

Red Dove's mouth opened, but no sound came out.

"Stand up, Mary. Go ahead and tell everyone what you've done and why you did it."

Red Dove rose to her feet, knees shaking. She stared at the pews full of wide-eyed, anxious girls.

"It wasn't me," Red Dove managed to croak.

"You're lying, you insolent girl. The two of you were in it together. That's my second announcement. I caught you red-handed with the third accomplice: Sister Mary Rose—"

"It isn't true!" shouted Red Dove

"Quiet," warned Sister Agatha. "So as of this morning, Sister Mary Rose is dismissed. Immediately."

Stunned gasps followed.

"She'll be sent back to Ireland. And we won't have to put up with her insolence—or her stupidity—again," Sister Agatha said with a satisfied smirk.

>> Sitting Bull is Dead <<

Red Dove lingered in the chapel, waiting for Sister Agatha's return. She breathed in the smells of Christmas, only days away, and stared up through the high arched windows, trying to imagine the road Sister Mary Rose would take. Ireland, she thought. How far is that?

She reached up for the pouch, and remembered: it was still hidden, stuffed under the mattress of her bed.

"You're in terrible danger," someone said.

Danger? Who is?

Red Dove turned her head to see through the open door of the chapel. There in the hall stood Jerusha, surrounded by Sister Agatha and a flock of squawking nuns.

"Silence, all of you," Sister Agatha said, frowning at Jerusha. "Just tell us what you know."

"The Indians are on the warpath. They could attack any moment—"

"Ach du lieber Gott!" cried Sister Gertrude.

"You've got to get the children out of here; let them go back to their families where they'll be safe," Jerusha went on.

"Just tell us what happened," Sister Agatha answered in a steely tone.

"It was the ghost dancing," Jerusha said breathlessly. "The reservation agent thought it was stirring the Indians up, so he ordered Sitting Bull to put a stop to it. But Sitting Bull wouldn't. Or couldn't. And the Indian police, the ones who work for the soldiers, went to his cabin and arrested him. But he wouldn't go, so they shot him, and he's dead—"

Red Dove rushed up.

"*There* you are my dear. I was so worried." Relief flooded Jerusha's face as she opened her arms. "But why are you in your nightdress? You look sick. That's it. I'm taking both you and your brother home—"

"You can't." Sister Agatha's eyes narrowed. "All the children are staying with me. They're as safe here as anywhere and here they will remain."

"But Sister—"

"Nonsense." Sister Agatha turned, raised her wooden rosary beads to her pursed lips and stared through the window. "If the children are here, the warriors are less likely to attack," she said in a calm, even tone.

"Less likely to attack... attack *you*, you mean?" Jerusha said, her voice pitching higher.

"The Indians won't harm their own—"

"So you'll use the children as *hostages*? For *shame*. How dare you?"

"And how dare you speak to me that way," said Sister Agatha, her eyes glinting dangerously.

Jerusha's eyes raked the hall. "And where's her brother? Where's Walks Alone? What have you done with him?"

"He's run away—"

"*Run away?* Dear God, is *no one* safe with you?" Jerusha straightened her spine and clenched her little fists.

"That's enough," said Sister Agatha, towering over her. "We don't need any more trouble—"

"Oh, *I'll* give you trouble." Jerusha glared up at the nun. "I'll see that you're called up by the authorities, that you're punished—"

"For what?" Sister Agatha said with a smirk.

"For endangerment of the children—"

"Endangerment?" Sister Agatha laughed. "These are dangerous times, and you think *I'm* endangering them? Our best security *is* the children. If they stay here, then no one will get hurt."

"I've never heard anything so outrageous, using children to protect yourself. Surely—" Jerusha swiveled her head from nun to nun, searching for support.

But there wasn't any. One by one, the nuns turned their frightened faces away.

Jerusha looked at Red Dove. "We *will* find your brother, won't we? That's the least we can do. And if he's run away, I'm sure he had plenty of reason… and will have stories to tell about the way he's been treated here," she said, glaring at the nuns.

"What do you mean by that?" asked Sister Agatha.

"Things my brother heard." Jerusha turned back to Red Dove and grabbed her arm. "So you're coming with me."

"No!" The heel of Sister Agatha's boot came down against the floor. "They belong to me. You saw the document. They were placed in my care."

"I saw some papers—"

"That gave me the authority," said Sister Agatha, smiling grimly.

Red Dove looked from one to the other. Do something, she begged silently.

Jerusha blinked in confusion. Then, suddenly, her

shoulders slumped and she let go of Red Dove. "Ah, my dear, I'm so sorry, but the law *is* the law—"

"It is." Sister Agatha nodded towards the door. "So now I suggest you leave immediately. For your safety as well as ours."

"Don't go," Red Dove blurted.

"I have to. There's nothing else I *can* do, my dear." Jerusha reached inside her sleeve, pulled out a handkerchief and dabbed at her nose. "And maybe it's true your people wouldn't hurt you and you *will* be safer here."

"I'll be safer at home."

Jerusha touched Red Dove's arm. "Thomas and I will do everything we can to find poor Walks Alone—"

"You can't leave me," said Red Dove, shaking her head.

"I have to, my dear. I have no choice." said Jerusha.

"Because of a piece of paper?"

"It's the law; don't you see?" Jerusha reached out again, but Red Dove pulled away.

Jerusha gave a sad little smile and tucked her handkerchief back inside her sleeve. "I have to go now. And when all this is over, I *will* be back... and there *will* be a reckoning," she said, raising her chin and narrowing her eyes at Sister Agatha. Then she reached out to give Red Dove one last pat before turning on her heel and starting the long, slow walk down the hall, hard soles clacking against the floor.

≫ Walks Alone ≪

Red Dove's first Christmas came and went. The ceremonies were elaborate, the decorations colorful, the smells exotic, but the days were cold and cheerless with the school still under siege, barricaded against attack. The smell of fear was in the air.

"Back to work," said Sister Agatha after the holidays were over. She clapped her hands to scatter the gaggle of nuns. "And you, there," she said to Red Dove, pointing to the kitchen.

Red Dove stumbled into the empty room. She stared at the piles of dishes waiting in the sink, the pots sitting on the soot-blackened stove, the remains of a joyless feast. Then she looked through the window at the fields beyond.

Who's left to lead us now that Sitting Bull is dead?

"Grandfather?" she whispered, desperate for an answer. "Can you hear my words, can you hear my thoughts? Are you listening... ? Maybe not, since I'm no longer using this." She felt for the pouch she had stuffed back in her pocket, brought it out, and sniffed the familiar earthy smell. On impulse, she reached up and tied it round her neck.

"Grandfather?" she whispered and closed her eyes.

A circle of lodges in a village like her own.

Drumming, chanting, dancers all around, dressed in blue-painted shirts covered with symbols: stars and fish and birds. Swaying to the music, for minutes, or hours or days—impossible to tell—and darkness coming and going. Dancers falling, one by one, intoxicated by hunger and exhaustion and the power of the drum.

Like the ghost dancers I saw that day.

Soldiers on the hill above, dragging heavy cannon into place.

Daylight. Cannon black against a morning sky. Soldiers sprawled on the ground in the center of the lodges, sleeping around a keg of whisky, snoring and muttering in a drunken doze, waking to a bugle call, cursing and muttering and shielding their eyes from the harsh winter light.

An old warrior, head wrapped in a white scarf, walking out of his tepee, raising his pipe to the soldiers. "We come in peace."

"Give up your weapons then, Spotted Elk."

"We have."

"Gonna make one more search to be sure."

Soldiers moving from tepee to tepee, grabbing anything sharp or pointed or blunt and hard. A pile of rusted firearms, cooking knives and pots and pans growing in the camp.

A soldier pointing to a bewildered old man. "That Indian over there. What's he got under his blanket? Looks like a gun—"

The old warrior pointing to his ear. "He cannot hear you."

"Deaf you say? Then we'll make him understand."

A shot ringing out. Cannon firing from the ridge. Soldiers on horseback thundering into the camp. Smoke filling the air.

A woman, a baby at her breast, racing for the trees, a bullet reaching her as she falls to the ground, clutching her child.

Three little boys running towards a ditch. "Mihakup ooh!" *the oldest crying. "Follow me." His brothers hurling themselves in, crouched and waiting, gunshots finding them all.*

A young warrior in a painted blue shirt turning to face the cannon... .

"Walks Alone!" Red Dove, screaming now, reaching towards him, her legs not moving.

Panicking, frozen in a cloud of dust and grit. A horse thundering up, hooves drowning out the sounds around. Noise fading, blending into a steady hum, a constant thump, thump, thump.

A heartbeat?

A rush, a crash and being lifted, carried up, exploded through a tunnel... and out the other side.

And understanding: the heartbeat, the eyes she is seeing through, the rage and fear and courage she is feeling are those of someone else —her brother Walks Alone.

I'm living through him.

Something slamming against her chest.

Falling, tasting dirt and blood, lying there helpless, staring at a winter sky... .

Red Dove forced her eyes open, trying to escape the terrifying vision. A beam of light from a high window blinded her and she had to shut her eyes once again before she could drag herself to where her body really was—collapsed on the hard cold stone of a boarding school kitchen. She rose slowly and walked to the window. And there in the distance was a dusty gray cloud, hovering over the road, gathering size and moving swiftly towards to the school. Terror gripped her as she remembered the cannon on the hill, the bullets, the metal taste of blood.

Soldiers! And they're coming... after us!

>> It Should'a Been Easy <<

Red Dove ran blindly down the hall and made a desperate lunge for the huge front door, trying to get away—but it was locked, barricaded against attack.

She heard a voice. *"Look in the church."*

She ran to the chapel, glanced past the empty pews to the carved nativity scene, still garlanded for Christmas.

A mother, a father, a child... in a stable, Red Dove thought. *They found safety, so I can too... but where? The door is locked, the windows are too high.*

She heard a noise from the courtyard and glanced at the side door. It was open.

Heart beating wildly, she raced through and stepped outside as the first wagon, loaded with men in torn and bloodied uniforms, rolled in.

She backed behind a pillar. Hidden in a pool of blue shadow, she watched as soldiers slid from weary horses to help the men staggering from the wagons.

She jumped at a voice behind her. "Terrible ain't it? Warn't nothin' but a massacre. A filthy, hellish massacre."

Red Dove turned to face a red-bearded man slumped against the wall. His uniform was torn and bloodied, his voice trembled and his red-rimmed eyes held hers for a moment before he lowered them and spat in the dirt.

Should I run? She touched her pouch and watched his face, looking for the thoughts inside his head. And saw what he saw:

Wagons, filled with young and old... people like her, covered with blood.

"It should'a been easy," he mumbled, looking at Red Dove before averting his eyes again. "We drank too much, 'cause we knew we was safe—that old chief couldn't fight; he was our captive and he was sick. But the orders from the general was clear: 'Disarm 'em' he said. 'Do everythin' you can to make sure the Indians don't escape. And if they fight, destroy 'em.' So we did... just needed one more weapons check to make sure. But why was they so slow to hand 'em over? What was they thinking? And that deaf one—he wouldn't give up his gun.... Didn't he know we had rifles and cannon, that he had no chance? And who fired first? Us or them?"

It's what I saw in my dream, Red Dove realized, as she watched him sway slightly and steady himself against the post.

"All that killin'" the soldier went on. "Women, children, even our own men caught in the crossfire. It shouldn't 'a been like that."

It shouldn't, Red Dove thought. And whose fault is that?

Tears rolled down his beard as Red Dove listened to him tell what he remembered. She felt his disgust, knew that he would spend the rest of his life with the terrible memory.

Good, she thought.

"Are you hurt, soldier?" Sister Agatha called from across the courtyard.

Red Dove jumped behind the pillar.

"What?" The soldier wiped his face with his sleeve.

"I asked if you were hurt."

"No, but some of my men may be. They've had a bad time of it. Need water." He lurched towards the chapel, stumbled up over the threshold and disappeared inside.

Sister Agatha eyed him suspiciously. "Sister Gertrude," she ordered, clapping her hands. "See to these men. Now." Then her eyes found Red Dove. "And take Mary with you," she said with a slow smile. "Make sure she doesn't get away."

>> A Holy Place <<

Sister Gertrude marched up to Red Dove, grabbed her by the sleeve and pulled her back into the chapel. "Don't chust stand zere. Be useful."

Inside, soldiers were everywhere. Some were wounded, some just dazed, lying on pews or on the cold stone floor in dusty, bloodied uniforms. One walked unsteadily towards them. "Goddam Indian." He pointed at Red Dove.

Sister Agatha's voice rose above the din. "Who said that?"

"She *is* an Indian, ain't she?" growled the soldier.

Red Dove saw Sister Agatha's nose twitch—and knew what would come. "She is, but it's what you said before that.

I won't have you cursing in a holy place. Leave immediately," Sister Agatha said in an icy voice.

"Ah, come on, I didn't mean no harm—"

"Leave. Now."

The man ripped his battered hat off his head and hugged it to his chest. "Didn't mean no disrespect, ma'am—"

"Sister."

"Sister. We need help is all, after what we been through."

What *you've* been through? thought Red Dove, remembering the images from her dream.

The soldier raised his eyes to Sister Agatha for a moment, then slid them away when he saw the expression in hers. "Awright," he said finally and stumbled out, slamming the door so hard it swung back on its hinges with a bang.

"Did I make myself clear? There will be no disrespect," said Sister Agatha.

Men nodded and mumbled in agreement.

"She tell zem," said Sister Gertrude admiringly. Then she pointed to a skinny old soldier lying on the ground. "Take his feet."

Red Dove grabbed the old man's ankles and, struggling, she and Sister Gertrude hoisted him up and onto the nearest pew. The man moaned, flicked his eyes open for a moment and smiled.

"He doesn't seem wounded," whispered Red Dove.

"Vounded?" snorted Sister Gertrude. "He is *besoffen*... drunk." She held her nose with her fingertips. "*Schrecklich.* Terrible." She brushed her hands on her apron and crossed herself. "Stay here. I get vater."

Red Dove turned to stare through the open doorway

at the courtyard, now thronged with men and wagons and horses. Hitched to the rail was a brown and white Indian pony, a mare, bobbing her shaggy head and gazing at her.

"Take me," she seemed to say.

>> Her First Precious Moments of Freedom <<

Ignoring Sister Gertrude's order and making sure she was unseen, Red Dove bounded up the long staircase and into the empty dormitory. She crouched under her bed, pulled up the loose floorboards and grabbed the bundle of clothes hidden underneath. Her deerskin robe was stiff from lack of use, but its musty smell brought comfort, so she tore off her cotton pinafore, thin gray dress and hard leather shoes and pulled the familiar garment over her head. She ripped off her shoes, shoved her feet in her moccasins and reached for her blanket and *parfleche*.

My pouch... She reached up to make sure it was still tied around her neck. It was.

She crept unseen down the stairs and into the empty kitchen. She grabbed an earthenware jug, filled it with water and plugged it with a stopper. Pulling open the cupboard, she found two loaves of bread and stuffed them in the bag.

Something thudded to the floor: an apple, the first she had seen since she came to the school. She picked it up, dropped it in her *parfleche* and raced to the hall, just as Sister Agatha came around the corner. "Where do you think you're going?"

Away from here, Red Dove wanted to scream.

"I'm... getting water... for the soldiers," she mumbled instead, holding up the jug.

"Dressed like that?" The nun's eyes glinted.

"It's... safer this way... if the warriors attack. If we're dressed in our own clothes, they'll see who we are, so they won't hurt us... or you."

Sister Agatha squinted at Red Dove, her wispy brows crawling like caterpillars above her eyes. Then a slow grin lifted the corners of her mouth. "Clever, aren't you? Come here." She pointed to the stove.

"Why?" Red Dove reached up to touch her pouch.

"What is that you have under your collar? Some sort of heathen wickedness, no doubt. Let me see. We'll get rid of it—"

"No." Red Dove closed her hand over the pouch.

"Come here, I said!" Sister Agatha yanked Red Dove by the sleeve and pulled her towards the cast iron stove that still smoked from the midday meal. She grabbed the poker with one hand and jerked open the heavy door with the other. "Throw it in."

Red Dove saw the embers, smoldering from gold to red and fear coursed through her.

Sister Agatha thrust the poker into the coals and the iron began to smoke. "Witchcraft, is it?" she said, narrowing her eyes. "It'll soon be gone. This fire's hot enough." She pulled the poker from the embers and held it up. It glowed a dull red. "Open your collar. Throw whatever it is in. Now."

Red Dove heard the voices in her head. *"No, no, no,"* they said.

"No," she echoed.

"Do as I say." Sister Agatha grabbed Red Dove's collar, tore it open and stepped back, a look of amazement on her face. "But... there's nothing there. Nothing but a strip of leather tied around your neck. That's all. What kind of fool do you take me for?" Her eyes blazed with fury as she ripped the leather tie from Red Dove's neck and the little pouch Sister Agatha couldn't see fell to the ground.

Red Dove bolted, grabbed the pouch and raced down the hallway, past the startled nuns, and out through the courtyard. She untied the pony from the rail, threw herself on its shaggy back and burst through the gate.

"Take me far away from here," she cried as she tasted her first precious moments of freedom.

≫ You're Comin' with Us ≪

Daylight waned and the sky turned a sullen gray as Red Dove and the pony rode on, trying to find the road to her village.

I left my village during the Moon-of-Ripe-Plums, she thought, and now it's the Moon-of-Popping-Trees, when ice crackles on the tree branches. My family will have moved to find shelter in the Black Hills. And that's where Walks Alone is too, probably, so that's where I'll look.

Fat flakes fell and darkness closed in as a full moon began to rise. Still clinging to the shaggy back, Red Dove breathed in the horsey smell and scanned the colorless landscape. "I have a blanket and food and water. And I have you," she said, bending close to the pony's ear. "So it's just you and me now, girl," she whispered, slowing the animal to a trot. "Girl… you are a girl, aren't you, like me? And a pretty one… so maybe that's what I'll call you. Pretty Girl… *Wichinchala*."

The pony tossed her head.

"You like that name, don't you—"

She saw something up ahead, moving swiftly. She pulled

Wichinchala to a stop and struggled to see through the frozen light.

Wagons... Soldiers!

She searched for a place to hide, but there was none, and the convoy was moving fast. Before Red Dove could turn and run, it closed around her.

Rigid with fear, she waited as the riders passed her by, ignoring a lone young girl on a small brown and white pony.

"Leave 'er be," one of the men called. "She ain't no harm to us."

As the last wagon drew near, she saw who was in it: a boy slumped on the seat in front, and a one-eyed man holding the reins beside him.

The ones from the fort... the boy who threw the rock and the man who kicked his dog... please, please don't let them notice me. Red Dove pulled her blanket up to hide her face.

"Hey, get outta the road," shouted the man, jerking the wagon to a halt beside her.

Red Dove froze. She didn't answer.

"Where ya headed?" he said, pulling out his gun and aiming it at her.

"To... my family," she stammered.

"Not any more, y'aint."

Red Dove stared at the gun. And heard a click.

"Don't, Jake!"

"Shut up, Rick," growled the man, jabbing the boy with his elbow. "A hostage'll come in handy." He eyed her appraisingly. "So you're comin' with us." With his free hand, he grabbed Wichinchala's reins and handed them to Rick. "Hang on to 'em so she don't go nowhere."

"Sure, Jake," said Rick, not looking at Red Dove as he did as he was told.

Numb with cold and fear, Red Dove sat on Wichinchala, following alongside. They continued straight for what seemed hours, Jake nodding off and then jerking awake, letting the horses lead the way, until at last something loomed in the distance, blacker than the leaden sky.

The fort?

A smell hit her nostrils: the sick-sweet stench of summer plums, rotting in the sun. Why? It's not summer; there are no plums... Is the pouch trying to tell me something?

"Cold ain't it?" The boy squeaked, leaning close to her and away from Jake. She could barely see his face in the darkness. "Cold, ain't it?" he repeated, an octave lower. "Name's Rick. What's yours?" he whispered.

Red Dove shook her head.

"Not gonna tell me, huh?

"It's *Wakiyela Sa*," she said with a shrug.

"Waki what?"

"Red Dove. In your language."

"Nice. Where was you goin', Red Dove?"

"To my people."

"Your people, huh?" Rick laughed. "That ain't where you're headed now, is it? Where'd you come from? You got short hair an' speak English like you been to school, but you're not dressed like any schoolgirl I seen."

"I'm going to search for my family," Red Dove repeated, finding her courage now that she was no longer staring at the barrel of a gun.

"Maybe you don't wanna go lookin' for 'em right now." The

smile faded from Rick's face. "Gettin' colder," he mumbled, and hunched his shoulders. "So just forget I said anythin'."

I will, thought Red Dove, pulling her fingers from the pouch so she wouldn't have to learn any more.

>> Where's Your Dog <<

In the distance, the gates of the fort opened, sinister and strange, as they covered the last few miles on the rutted, snowy road.

Is this where I was before? It looks so different.

Red Dove searched her memory and again was struck by the sweet stench of rotting plums. That was summer, and this is winter... what is the pouch trying to tell me?

She raised her fingers to her throat.

"Why do you keep touchin' your neck like that?" asked Rick. "This here's where we live," he went on, nodding at a row of lighted windows that dotted the walls around the fort. "We're soldiers," he said, smiling broadly.

Red Dove didn't answer.

"Don't say much, do you?" he grunted. The glow from a lamp pole lit his darkly tanned cheeks, his disheveled auburn hair. "You don't need to be afraid. I won't let 'em hurt you. I'll make sure you get food and a place to sleep."

"You don't need to," she started to say—then stopped abruptly as his amber eyes found hers. She felt something stir inside her. "Where's your dog?" she blurted.

"How'd ya know I had one?" he asked.

"I saw you once. Here at the fort... I think."

"Yeah? When?"

"When I was here with my mother. Trading." Red Dove

raised her eyes to his. "You threw a rock at me."

"Oh." He ducked his head. "That was you? I shouldn'ta done it. Sorry... You all right?" he muttered.

"I'm fine. So where is your dog?"

"Dunno." There was a catch in Rick's voice as he turned his head away.

Red Dove stared at his profile: his copper-colored hair, the skin at the back of his neck, deep-tanned even in winter. She felt for her pouch and watched him remember the animal's scruffy fur, his wolf-like snout and yellow, close-set eyes.

The wagon jerked to a stop. "Rick, go find some place to put her," Jake barked.

"Yessir." Rick gave Red Dove a quick smile, slid from his horse and started shuffling across the frozen ground to the barracks. "Wait here. I'll be back."

He's sorry, Red Dove thought, her fingers curled tight around the pouch, so... maybe I'll help him find his dog.

And then she remembered. He's a soldier, he threw a rock at me, and my ankle still hurts... so no, she decided and pulled her blanket tight against the cold.

>> Safe From the Storm <<

One by one, the windows surrounding the fort began to glow as men straggled into the barracks. Red Dove, stiff from exhaustion, sat on her pony, waiting. The sky turned black, the stars covered by clouds, and from the heaviness in the air, she knew the weather would get worse. She pulled her blanket over her head as Wichinchala, cold, hungry and tied to the rail, snorted in protest.

"Shhh," Red Dove pleaded, patting the animal's ice-covered mane. "Just a little while longer."

She looked at the barred gate and the sentry high atop the tower. I should try to escape, but how? I'm hungry, I'm cold and I'm exhausted. And I could get lost in the dark. I'll wait til morning.

Snow fell harder, and still no one came. Through the lighted windows, Red Dove saw soldiers around a table, leaning back in their chairs, laughing and shouting.

That's enough, she thought. She slipped off Wichinchala, edged round the ice-covered puddles and stepped up onto the slippery plank walkway.

Then she knocked at the door. No one answered, so she knocked again.

"Heard ya the first time," hollered a voice. There was a rattle of cups, the scrape of a chair against the floor and the click of a latch being drawn. A scruffy old soldier stood before her, dark against the light, red suspenders dangling from dirty rumpled pants. "Whatcha want?"

"I—"

"It's an Indian," he said, turning to the men at the table. "Anyone want 'er?"

"Dangit, Rick!" shouted Jake, throwing his cards on the table. "You was s'posed to take care of 'er."

"I tried," answered Rick, jumping up from a bunk in the corner. "But you wouldn't let me. Every time I started to go help her, you stopped me."

"Do whatever ya like. Just get rid of 'er so she don't go interruptin' our game." Jake picked up his cards again. Rick looked at Red Dove and shrugged. "Sorry."

"Get rid of her, I said!" Jake threw down his cards, walked

over and shoved Rick outside. Then he slammed the door on both of them.

"This way, I guess," mumbled Rick, staring at his feet. Coatless, he shivered in the cold.

At least I have a blanket, she thought. "Is he always like that to you?"

"Yeah. But it ain't so bad. I report to the cap'n, an' he's good to me."

Red Dove reached up to touch her pouch and look into his thoughts. She saw he was lying: the captain couldn't always protect him. "What about my pony?" she asked, to change the subject.

"It's an Indian pony, ain't it? With that shaggy coat it don't need to be inside—"

"But I want to stay with her—"

"Then tether her in there." Rick pointed to a stable at the far end of the courtyard, barely visible in the dim light. "An' you can sleep there, too. There's straw and water an' you got a warm blanket. I'll find you some food in the mornin'." His amber eyes reflected the light from the lamp. "Listen, I'm real sorry we left you out here in the cold so long. I tried to tell 'em that we shouldn't treat you like that."

"I know."

"Heck. Well, go on then," he muttered, slapping his arms against his chest. "Get inside where it's warm."

Red Dove untied Wichinchala from the wagon and guided her to the stable. The door creaked on its hinges when she opened it and the smell of horses hit her nostrils.

Safe for now, she thought, leading her pony to an empty stall and brushing her face against the animal's soft neck. But we have a long way to go before we're home—wherever that is.

She picked up a handful of hay and held it up to the pony's muzzle. The little horse extended her neck gracefully and nibbled.

"You're probably thirsty, too," said Red Dove. Squinting against the dark, she found an ice-filled bucket. "Hope this is clean." She made a fist and punched through the frozen crust to the liquid beneath. Cupping her hand, she raised it to her nose. Smells okay, she thought, and took a sip. Then she hoisted the bucket close to the pony's muzzle and watched her drink.

At last, Red Dove burrowed deep into the sweet-smelling hay that lined the stall, her blanket tight against the cold, and finally fell into the delicious sleep she craved.

A woman's voice broke the stillness. *"Rushes, straw, bring whatever you can to soak this up."*

What... who's there?

Red Dove sat up, opened her eyes and looked around. No one. She peered up at the hayloft. Still no one. She closed her eyes and fell back down again, fearing that sleep wouldn't come. But it did. And with it came a dream.

Evergreen boughs covering an altar. The smells of Christmas mingled with a sharper scent rising from the rush-covered floor. A frail little white woman moving carefully around bodies lying there, dabbing at her eyes with a tattered gray rag, using it to soak up the pools of sticky liquid from the floor, muttering to herself. "Butchers."

Who are they? Where am I? In a church?

The old woman moving awkwardly around the broken limbs, the bandaged wounds, the suffering in the faces of the bodies lying there.

They're dressed like people from my village… but it can't be real.

Red Dove forced her eyes open to remind herself where she really was—alone with animals in a stable.

"Grandfather?" she croaked. "Tell me what I'm seeing."

She listened for a response, but all she heard was the sighing of the wind blowing through the cracks in the wall. "Can you hear me?" she tried again. "Tell me what it is, so I can understand."

But her mind was too weary, her body too spent, and instead of waiting for an answer, she closed her eyes again and fell into a dreamless sleep.

>> It's So Cold <<

A shaft of moonlight crept through a chink in the wall. Red Dove opened her eyes and pulled the blanket closer.

Almost dawn, but still dark enough to escape—and go find my family.

She knew where they would be: not in the village she had left, but in *Paha Sapa*, the Black Hills, their winter home.

She rose to her feet, ran her fingers through her tangled hair and stumbled to the door. Using all her strength, she pulled at the frozen latch. It gave with a groan. The courtyard, a mass of mud and freezing water the night before, was now a field of purest white.

She turned to the pony and offered a handful of hay. Then she opened her *parfleche*. "Not much… but here." She laid the apple on her palm and stretched it out to the animal. "For you," she said. "It's what they promised at the school, but I never got one. So I don't like them anymore." She tore off a chunk of dry bread and ate that instead.

Walking to the door and heaving it open, she forced a gap wide enough for them both.

"Time," she whispered, slinging her *parfleche* over her shoulder. Noiselessly, she guided the little mare through the opening and across the frozen courtyard up to the heavy gate. And saw the sentry slumped in the tower.

Asleep? Good.

Pushing with all her might, she hoisted the heavy crossbeam off its iron braces. It fell to the ground with a thud.

That'll wake them, she thought with alarm and shoved open the gate.

"Who's there?" cried the sentry. Climbs onto pony's back after opening gate.

But Red Dove was on her pony's back and through before he could take aim.

"We're going home, Wichinchala—to find Mother and Grandfather and Walks Alone. And this time just let them *try* to stop us!"

>> You're Comin' With Me <<

Red Dove slowed her pony to a walk, searching for the road. It was almost morning now, but snow still fell in a hard, heavy fall that erased the line between earth and sky.

"Hey," came a shout from behind.

Rick!

Red Dove dug her heels into the pony's firm flank. "Yah," she yelled, "yah, yah, yah." She kicked Wichinchala to a gallop, but the thunder of hooves grew louder as Rick, on his bigger mount, caught up.

"Where d'you think you're goin'?" he yelled, coming

alongside and grabbing Wichinchala's reins.

"I told you. My people."

"Yeah, an' I told you you might not find 'em," said Rick, jerking her pony to a halt.

"I *won't*, if you don't let me go—"

"That's not what I mean," Rick said, suddenly serious. "You might not want to find 'em… if they were there."

"Where?"

"Up ahead. Don't go." He looked away. "You won't like what you see."

Red Dove touched her pouch. She saw Rick's face, clear in the morning light, and watched as his memories began to form.

It was the same vision she had had before, the same slaughter she had seen in her dream. "That wasn't my village," she whispered. "Those weren't my people—"

"Sure hope you're right. 'Cause I don't think you want to go to Wounded Knee Creek."

She remembered what had frightened her most in the dream: the sight of her brother turning to face the guns.

"Either way, you're comin' with me."

"I am not." Red Dove grabbed the reins from his hand.

"You have to. You're my captive." Rick reached for his gun.

A stab of fear ran through Red Dove. She saw his hand reach for the holster. And come up empty.

Relief flooded through her. She dug hard with her heels and galloped past him, towards the hills, barely visible in the snow.

"Hey!" called Rick, from behind. "You know I can't go back without you."

"Then *you* come with me."

"What?"

"Come with me. To where *I'm* going."

"Aw heck," cried Rick, closing the gap between them. "Where is that?"

"You'll find out," she said.

>> Captive <<

The hiss of falling snow was drowned by the steady thud of hooves as the sun came out and warmed the day. Rick rode a length ahead of Red Dove. "Smoke ahead. See it? Gettin' close to town, I think, where they'll have food and water. But you better let me do the talkin'."

Red Dove didn't argue. They had a better chance of finding help if a white man asked for it.

Rick handed back the reins and took the lead again.

They rode through the slushy street, past a shuttered storefront and an empty saloon.

"Town ain't woke up yet," Rick muttered. "But *they're* awake." He pointed to smoke curling from a squat little cabin opposite a white-painted church. The road that led to it was slick with ice and slush. A dog yapped as they rode by.

Rick brought his mare to a halt and tied her to the fence in front of the cabin. "Wait here," he said and pulled at the snow-covered gate. It gave with a shower of flakes. He crossed the yard, climbed up on the porch and knocked on the door.

And knocked again. "Nobody home," he muttered, just as the door creaked open and a balding head appeared. "Whatcha want?"

"'Scuse me sir, but I'm escortin' a captive here." Rick

jerked his thumb at Red Dove, sitting on her pony. "An Indian. Army business. An' we need supplies. Can you spare some food and water?"

"Hmmm… ," said the man, scratching at the stubble on his chin. He squinted against the glare. "Army business? Don't wanna get mixed up in no trouble. Say," He pulled up his grimy denim pants and stepped onto the snowy porch to get a better look. "Don't I know you?" He smiled. "Why I'll be. It's you, ain't it? The girl from the village, the one I brung to the school?"

"*Han*, Old Tom," Red Dove replied, sliding off her pony onto the snowy ground. She tied Wichinchala to the fence alongside Rick's mare and picked her way carefully up through the snow.

"You know each other?"

"Known her people for years, son, so come on in." Old Tom waved them both through the door and into the house.

The small front room was spare but neat. Yellowed lace curtains hung from the window frame and a frayed linen cloth sat on top of a scrubbed wood table, the stillness broken only by the ticking of a longcase clock in the corner.

"They cut your hair, I see. Pity," he said to Red Dove. "But Jerusha ain't with you? She was headed back to get you. Left a while ago. "

"She *did* come to the school," said Red Dove. "But that was before Christmas."

"She was gonna try again. Thought now the holidays was over and things had died down a bit, they'd let 'er." Old Tom shook his head. "Stubborn, that one. Never gives up on anythin'. Once she gets going, she's a hard woman to stop."

Good, thought Red Dove. Maybe I was wrong about her.

"Who's this?" Old Tom jerked a thumb at Rick.

"My captive, sir," Rick answered, stamping the snow from his boots. "She's a runaway."

"Runaway, huh?" said Old Tom, amused. "Well, good for her," he snorted. "Got a look at that place myself. Grim. You really mean to bring her back?"

"He's taking me to find my family." Red Dove narrowed her eyes at Rick, daring him to disagree.

"Kinda makes me wonder who captured who," said Old Tom, "and who's the runaway here—"

"Not me, sir," said Rick. "I'm on duty."

"Sure y'are, son. I didn't mean to imply you was absent without leave or nothin'."

"No, sir," said Rick. "Absolutely not, sir!"

But Red Dove, touching her pouch, saw the truth. He *is* running away from something: *Jake.*

"What say we go see what Jerusha's left us to eat." Old Tom shooed a small orange cat off the table and pulled up two chairs, scraping them against the floor. "You two must be starved." He went to the cupboard and took out a loaf of coarse brown bread and a small earthenware jar. "Help yourselves."

Rick reached for the bread, cut himself a thick slice and spread it with a gob of purple jam. Then he pushed the jar towards Red Dove. "Good," he mumbled through a mouthful of food.

"Jam's Jerusha's specialty. Makes it from the plums that grow wild around here."

No more plums for me, Red Dove thought, pushing the jar away and reaching for the bread.

A smile curled Old Tom's lip as he watched the young people eat.

Rick wiped his mouth on his sleeve and pushed his chair back from the table. "Thanks. We best be goin'," he said, before Red Dove was finished.

"Can't leave before Jerusha gets back. She'd never forgive me. She'll want to know what happened to you," Old Tom said, squinting at Red Dove. "So where is it you're *really* headed? Back to the school?"

"No sir," Rick answered. "To the fort."

Red Dove shook her head. "We're going to find my mother and my grandfather," she said, as firmly as she could. "And my brother too. He ran away."

"Things are gettin' mighty complicated." Old Tom scratched his stubble. "An' you're gonna have a hard time findin' your people in the dead of winter. They left their summer camp a while ago. Prob'ly headed to *Paha Sapa*, though it's hard to say for sure. Everythin's different now with all the fightin' an' they could be anywhere."

Disappointment darkened Red Dove's mood as she watched Old Tom carry Rick's plate to the sink.

"It's still none too safe to be travelin'," Old Tom called over his shoulder. "So what say we all jus' stay put and wait for Jerusha to get home. She may have news." He picked up Red Dove's plate and moved close to her ear. "That boy's a fool if he thinks you're *his* captive. More like he's *yours*."

Rick eyed them suspiciously. "Can you tell us what's ahead, sir? How bad it is, after the battle—"

"Weren't no battle." Old Tom aimed a wad of spit at the copper pot lying next to the table. "It was a godawful bloody slaughter."

Rick flinched. "I left before the fightin' started. Cap'n sent me away, so I never saw what happened. I just heard it was terrible."

"Yeah," said Old Tom with a wave. "It was. That's what I heard too. So like I said, let's wait for Jerusha to get home—"

The door opened with a creak. "An' here she is now."

>> What Did You Hear? <<

Jerusha burst through the door, ran up to Red Dove and threw her arms around her. "I am so glad to see you." She dropped her heavy satchel on the table and pulled off her damp shawl. "What happened?"

"I came on my own," said Red Dove.

"You ran away? Good." Jerusha's eyes shifted to Rick. "And who might you be?"

"Name's Rick Ryan, ma'am." Rick rose and extended his hand.

Jerusha pulled off her soggy bonnet, threw it on the table next to the satchel and extended her hand. "A soldier, I see."

"Yes ma'am. An' she's my captive."

"Captive? What's she done?" Jerusha asked with alarm.

"Run away."

"Is that all?" Jerusha tilted her head and smiled at Red Dove. "I'm glad you're out of there, papers or no papers—"

"Got any news for us, Sis?" Old Tom nodded at a corner of damp newsprint sticking out of the bag. "Whatcha learn?"

Jerusha gave Tom a meaningful look. "Just things. I'll tell you later."

There's something she doesn't want me to know, Red

Dove thought, as she watched Jerusha sink into a chair, put her elbows on the table and drop her face into her hands.

Red Dove touched her fingers to the pouch and started to read her thoughts, but Rick interrupted.

"I was there, ma'am," he said softly.

"Where?" asked Jerusha, raising her head to look at him.

"At Wounded Knee."

"You were there... at the massacre?" Jerusha's voice shook.

Rick shifted in his seat. "It wasn't a massacre exactly."

"It wasn't?" Jerusha's voice pitched higher. "What would you call it then, exactly?"

"I wasn't there, ma'am, but I heard... ." Rick looked to Old Tom for help.

"You heard? I thought you said you were there."

"Easy, Sis," Old Tom cautioned, but Jerusha ignored him.

"No, seriously; do tell us, young man," she said bearing down on Rick. "What is it *you're* doing here... *exactly*?"

"Leave the kid alone, Jerusha."

But Jerusha wouldn't stop. "This is too important, Thomas. This gentleman says he was there, so we have an eyewitness account. I want him to tell me in his own words what happened."

"Like I tried to say, ma'am," Rick said quietly, "I was there, but not when it happened—the fightin' I mean. I left before the shootin' started."

Jerusha eyed him suspiciously, took a breath and went on. "All right, then. What did you hear?"

"That it wasn't s'posed to go like it did. We jus' wanted to take the Indians' guns away. We wasn't s'posed to hurt 'em—"

"You weren't supposed to hurt them with *rifles and cannon*?

148

How could you not?"

Red Dove watched Rick's knee jerk up and down under the table.

He's trying not to cry, she thought.

"He's just a kid, Jerusha—" said Old Tom.

"And so is my brother," said Red Dove. "Has anyone seen *him*?" The room went silent and Red Dove stared at her empty mug, focusing on a crack near the handle as ugly thoughts raced through her head. "Maybe he was there," she whispered.

"I'll never forgive myself if he was," said Jerusha. "That horrible, horrible school. I wish to high Heaven I'd never brought you there. And now *this*." She flicked the newspaper.

"Stop it, Sis. You'll just get upset," said Old Tom.

"I *am* upset, Thomas. Why shouldn't I be? Why shouldn't we *all* be?" said Jerusha, with a fierce look in her red-rimmed eyes. Then she turned to Red Dove. "I am sorry, my dear. Truly sorry. For bringing you there. I never should have. And I want you to know we *will* find your brother, won't we, Thomas?"

"Course we will, Sis."

Jerusha nodded at the slim white spire, barely visible through the wavy glass of the little cabin window. "I've heard that they're taking some of the survivors to the church, so we should start looking there."

"So what's in that newspaper anyway, Sis? You gonna tell us?"

"Not now." Jerusha looked at Red Dove. "I hope you'll be warm enough with just that blanket, my dear, if we walk to the church."

She's changing the subject, Red Dove thought, because there's something in the newspaper she doesn't want me to know. She looked through the window. The morning brightness was blending into the coming light of day. She could see Wichinchala, still tied to the fence. "My pony—"

"Go put her in the stable. Thomas will help you."

"I'll do it," said Rick, leaping up and knocking over his chair. "Sorry," he muttered, picking it up again. "I'll make sure she's fed an' watered an' everythin'."

"Why thank you, young man," said Jerusha, raising an eyebrow. "Maybe you're not such a bad sort after all."

Red Dove saw the glow in his eyes. And felt a tiny thrill. Why am I feeling this way, when everything else is so terrible? she wondered.

>> Let's Go <<

Red Dove followed Rick out the door and onto the snow-covered porch. Something made her turn back around again. "You go ahead, Rick. I'll be right there."

"Sure," Rick said with a shrug and untied Wichinchala from the rail.

Red Dove pulled the door nearly shut, leaving a crack through which she could see Old Tom and Jerusha sitting at the worn wooden table, surrounded by four bark-covered walls.

Jerusha dropped a morsel of cheese onto the worn floorboards. "Here kitty, kitty," she called softly to the small orange cat who stretched herself across the windowsill and yawned.

"So what's in the paper, Sis?" Old Tom asked.

Jerusha didn't answer. Instead, she picked up her napkin and dabbed at her lips, eyes fixed on an elegant brass lamp that sat on the sideboard. "I don't know what I was thinking when I brought that from back East. It gives off such bright, clear light when there's whale oil to fill it, but we can never get any of that here. Just kerosene and these," she said, picking up a stub of yellow wax and stuffing it into a crude clay cup. "It gets so dark here, once summer's gone. But I'll have to get used to that."

"You're not answerin' the question, Sis, so somethin' must really be botherin' you. What's in that paper? I wanna know."

"All right." With a quick glance at the door, Jerusha pulled out the damp newspaper and spread it on top of the oak table. "See for yourself."

"Can't read it, Sis. Too wet," Old Tom said. "Writin's blurry."

"Oh Thomas," Jerusha sighed. She pushed her spectacles higher on her nose. "It's by that editor, L. Frank Baum. He writes children's books, I think."

"Jus' read it."

"Fine." Jerusha cleared her throat. "This is from the December 20 edition of the Aberdeen *Saturday Pioneer*. 'The Whites, by law of conquest, by justice of civilization, are masters of the American continent, and the best safety of the frontier settlements will be secured by the total annihilation of the few remaining Indians—'"

"Huh?" said Old Tom.

"That's what it says. Annihilation!"

What's that? Red Dove wondered. And then, reading Jerusha's thoughts, she knew—and felt as if someone had tied a stone around her waist and thrown her into a deep, black pool.

He wants us all dead.

"'Their glory has fled, their spirit broken, their manhood effaced,'" Jerusha went on, dropping her voice to a whisper, "'better they should die than live... .' Then he wrote this *after* the massacre: 'We had better, in order to protect our civilization, follow it up and wipe these untamed and untamable creatures from the face of the earth... .' Can you believe that? Wipe them from the face of the earth? He cannot mean it."

"Sounds like he can't bear to see people suffer, so he wants 'em to just disappear. Or else he's bein' sarcastic. Either way, it ain't right."

"No, Thomas, it isn't. But isn't it better to know the truth? And wouldn't we be doing the same thing by not reading it? Pretending it didn't exist, wanting it to disappear?"

"Mebbe. But I don't think you should read it to Red Dove."

"It would be too much, wouldn't it?" Jerusha's eyes strayed to the door. "They left the door open. It's freezing." She got up, walked over and caught sight of Red Dove standing behind it. "Oh no!" Jerusha shut the door and sat down.

Red Dove walked to the table and sank into a chair. No one moved. Afternoon shadows deepened as they sat in silence.

It was Old Tom who spoke, finally. "I think you *do* understand, don'tcha?" he said, leaning close to Red Dove with a searching look in his gentle blue eyes.

"Yes," said Red Dove.

Rick burst in, brushing snow from his pants and jacket. "Cold as heck out there," he said, "but the horses'll be warm though." He looked around. "Hey, what's goin' on?"

Jerusha took off her glasses and rubbed her eyes fiercely. Then she picked up a small copper plate and studied her reflection in the polished surface. "Right," she said, "that's it.

Who's coming?" She wiped her hands on her skirt.

"Where, Sis?"

"To the church. To help the survivors. Who's joining me?" she said, picking up her shawl and bonnet.

"Huh?"

"I am," said Red Dove.

"Me too, ma'am," said Rick, ducking his head with a shy smile at Red Dove.

"Thomas?" asked Jerusha.

"Why, well—why yeah, if you think it's the right thing."

"I do. Let's go."

>> Altar Cloth Bandages <<

Jerusha led the small party out of the cabin, across the slushy, sun-warmed street, and up to the door of the little white church. She knocked once, got no answer, turned the knob and pushed her way in.

A nightmare scene met their eyes. Sickened by the stench of blood and urine, Red Dove stared at the dark wooden beams and dingy whitewashed walls, still festooned with Christmas greenery and a banner that read "Peace on Earth, Good Will Toward Men."

A bushy-bearded soldier in a wrinkled uniform stumbled over bodies lying on the straw-covered floor. "This one's gone," he called to a weary-looking, old, gray-haired woman.

Gone... does he mean dead? wondered Red Dove.

"What can we do to help?" asked Jerusha, raising a handkerchief to her nose.

"Not much, I'm afraid." The soldier bent down and pulled a blanket over the face of a young woman. "She's beyond our help."

"Well, we have to do something. Put us to work, won't you?"

"Fine. Go fetch water. In the kitchen. There." The soldier nodded at a door, and Jerusha moved swiftly towards it.

Jerusha looked around the filthy room. "I'd better boil it first," she said.

Old Tom shuffled over to the gray-haired woman in a bloody apron, who hovered over a tiny girl. "Here, let me," said Old Tom.

The old woman looked up, startled, and nodded with gratitude in her weary eyes. "Thank you." She handed him a bowl of murky red water with a brown rag floating in it. "Bleeding's nearly stopped. But she can't drink because of the hole in her neck… water keeps seeping out. She'll die of thirst this way." The rest of her words were muffled as she choked back a sob. "Butchers."

"Here." Old Tom handed Red Dove the bowl of water. "Look after her." He led the frail old woman to a chair in the corner and lowered her into it. "Rest."

"Thank you. God bless you, I will," said the woman. "We're all so bone-weary tired. And there's no one here to help," she said, pushing a strand of gray off her face and looking around.

"Where's the doctor?" asked Old Tom.

"Doctor?" scoffed the woman. "*He's* come and gone. Said there was nothing he could do. It was the first time he'd seen women and children shot to pieces like this and he just couldn't take it."

Red Dove saw Rick watching in horrified silence. Do something, she thought, *anything*. But she herself didn't know what that should be. She knelt next to the little girl and dabbed at the wound with the blood-soaked rag.

"No more'n five or six years old, prob'ly," Old Tom muttered, walking back over.

The girl's eyes flicked open.

"*Aho*," he whispered to her.

The little mouth moved in response, but no sound came out.

Old Tom rose, shoulders shaking. "Bandages," he said through gritted teeth. He looked at Rick. "Hurry."

"Where should I get 'em?"

"Anywhere. Just get 'em. Now."

"Yessir." Rick gave an awkward salute and scurried over to the old woman. "Bandages?" he asked.

The woman motioned weakly to an open door. "Storage closet over there. Make 'em up yourself out of whatever you can find."

Rick stumbled to the closet. "Nothin' here but some old cloths."

"Altar cloths. Use those."

"Ain't that kinda against religion?"

"Killing people is against religion," the woman muttered. "God will understand."

Rick pulled out his knife, held it high, and stabbed at the worn linen until a mountain of bandages grew at his feet.

>> Walks Alone <<

The long hours left them all exhausted as they labored deep into the night. Wagons full of wounded kept arriving, and working tirelessly alongside the others, Red Dove watched

Jerusha, Old Tom and Rick drag buckets of water, fetch wood for the fire, and wrap bandages. The feeling of dread was back, the sensation of drowning in deep, cold water, sick and lost.

No. She covered her ears to block out the curses, the groans, the whispers flying around the room. I don't want to feel what other people are feeling. Not here, not now.

Blocking her ears didn't shut out another sound: a distant thrumming drone.

The pouch?

Her eyes fixed on the dimly lit corner. A native youth lay there, someone only recently brought in. The symbols on his blood-spattered, blue-painted tunic looked familiar, and when he turned his head, she saw.

"Walks Alone!" She hurled herself across the room.

He turned his head to meet her gaze and moved his lips, but all she heard was a hoarse whisper.

Falling to her knees, she touched her open palm to his chest. *Watching him, she heard what he heard, saw what he saw, felt what he felt: voices rising and falling in a room filled with murky light, the bite of blood and bile on his tongue. She felt his hideous pain.*

"He's alive," she screamed, waving wildly at Jerusha and Old Tom.

Jerusha broke away from the girl she was attending and rushed over. "Dear God!"

"Well I'll be," said Old Tom. "Thought we'd never see you again, son."

Eyes closed, Walks Alone turned his face weakly towards them.

"See if he'll take this." Jerusha's fingers shook as she

handed Red Dove the bowl of fresh water. When the cool liquid touched his mouth, Walks Alone's eyes opened again.

"You're safe now," Red Dove said in their language.

He shook his head. "They want to kill us all."

Red Dove listened to the buzzing, and saw again what he had seen: the blue-coated soldiers, the cannon on the hill, the bullet meant for him.

She felt a blow to her chest and a wave of pain swept over her.

I'm feeling what he felt… but no, this is worse. I'm living the experiences of all the people here, she thought, as the memories of those in the room became hers. Too many voices, too much hurt. She closed her eyes and began to sway.

"Red Dove? Are you all right?" Jerusha reached a hand to steady her. "You've been working too hard. You need rest."

"I need to go… outside… ." Red Dove stumbled up, her head filled with a deafening roar, her body racked with pain.

She staggered to the door—but before she could reach it, her knees crumpled and she fell, hard, onto the filthy, rush-covered floor.

>> He Was There <<

Red Dove awoke in an unfamiliar bed. It was full morning and a buttery light beat against her eyelids, making her head throb. She smelled the sweetness of bacon frying. Her stomach groaned.

How did I get here? she wondered.

The bed sheets were softer, smoother than the coarse homespun she remembered from the school. The pillow was fluffier, the blanket thicker. Everything here smelled fresh.

"Where am I?" she asked, Jerusha hovering over her.

"Home, my dear. With us." Jerusha nodded at Rick, who had walked in behind her. "You collapsed, you know. From exhaustion. There's a bruise on the side of your face, but nothing serious. How do you feel?"

"All right. I have to get back—"

"You will. We all will, but there are others in charge there now and they'll take care of things while we rest. In the meantime, I'll make you a nice cup of tea—"

"Walks Alone?" Red Dove said with a rush of remembering. "Where is he?"

"Here, my dear." Jerusha reached out to brush the stray hairs from Red Dove's forehead. "On a cot in the kitchen. We're taking care of him."

Red Dove sat upright. "I have to go to him."

"Of course you do, just not yet." Jerusha pushed her gently back down. "He's sleeping. You should rest, too."

"I have to." Red Dove pulled off the covers, dropped her feet to the floor and walked into the kitchen, where Walks Alone sat on his cot, propped up next to the black cast iron stove. He smiled weakly when he saw her.

"I'll leave you two alone then," Jerusha said, picking up the little orange cat and crossing into her bedroom.

"You seem better," Red Dove said.

"I am. I was lucky. The bullet knocked me down and broke a rib, but it wasn't serious. Just a flesh wound. What happened to you, Sister?" he asked, staring at the purple bruise across her cheek.

"I fainted and fell and hit my head, but I'm all right now."

Walks Alone patted the space next to him on the cot and Red Dove sat down.

"Mother? Grandfather?" she said, giving voice to the questions burning inside her, "did you find them?"

"Grandfather—" Walks Alone choked.

"What?"

"He was there—"

"At Wounded Knee? You saw him?"

"He came looking for me."

"He's alive? What happened?"

"I don't know," her brother said sadly. "I saw him, talked to him, and then... when the shooting started, I lost him."

Red Dove didn't want to think of what that meant. "And Mother?" she blurted.

"Stayed behind. With our people, Grandfather said."

"Where are they now, our people?"

"*Paha Sapa* I think, but I don't know." Walks Alone hung his head. "That's where Grandfather said they were going." His voice trailed off. "But he came to look for me, he said. He knew somehow that I had escaped from the school—"

"Maybe he's with the survivors then," said Red Dove, hoping that by saying the words, they would be true.

"I didn't see him."

"Jerusha says there are more wounded coming in so he might be with them. I'll go—"

"Where?" asked Jerusha, wiping her hands with a towel as she walked back into the room.

"To the church," said Red Dove. "To look for Grandfather. Walks Alone said he was there."

"There?" Jerusha frowned and then, nodding slowly, began to understand. "Oh... at Wounded Knee—then I'd better come, too."

>> Grandfather <<

Together, Red Dove, Jerusha and Rick plodded through the snowy yard, across the slushy street and up to the door of the church. It was full morning now, and Red Dove's eyes, blinded by sun reflecting off snow, couldn't see into the darkness inside. But she didn't need to see as she made her way slowly into the crowded room. She reached up and touched the pouch.

All the noises—the racking coughs, the angry curses, the desperate moans—blended into an ever-present drone.

I have to find him, she thought, and I need the pouch for that, but I don't want to feel what all the others are feeling. Not here, not now.

She tried to look away from the suffering faces, the ghastly wounds. Then she reached up, untied the pouch from around her neck, and stuffed it in her parfleche.

"Grandfather, where are you?" she whispered.

The drone continued, louder and louder as she moved farther into the room. It's trying to tell me something... It knows where Grandfather is.

She followed the drone to the darkest, dimmest corner of the church—and at last, she saw him, lying on a wrinkled blanket on the straw.

"Grandfather!" She rushed over and fell on her knees, trembling at the sight of his beloved old face.

Dressed for battle, an eagle feather in his thin gray hair, his clouded eyes searched hers. "You're not wearing the pouch."

It hurts too much, Grandfather.

"It is the pain of others you feel—"

I don't want to feel their pain.

"You must—if you want to understand—"

I don't want that. Not anymore.

"Ah, I see."

Grandfather, I'm sorry… I thought I was stronger, but I'm not. All I want now is to know how you are, so I can have you back again. That's all I care about.

A sad glint in the gentle eyes. "Then touch me—and you will know."

Leaning in and placing the flat of her palm against his narrow, bony chest. Feeling the pulsing of his heart, beating like a drum. Entering his thoughts: smelling the wood fire, the sacred healing smoke, seeing the dancers swaying in their painted shirts.

You were there at Wounded Knee, Grandfather?

"I was, Gray Eyes. I went to bring your brother home."

But you're both safe, so you'll be with us soon… won't you?

"The power is inside you now."

That's not an answer. We'll all be going home soon, won't we?

"The power is inside you now." His eyes glowing with a strange, otherworldly light. "Use it to find your happiness instead of pain."

How can I find happiness if all I feel is pain? That doesn't make any sense!

"It will." The voice began to fade. "And soon. But do something first… here."

Her throat ached and she wanted to wail the way she had as a child when things were too much to bear. Instead, Red Dove took a breath and let her eyes follow his finger, as it pointed to the little girl with the terrible wound.

Don't make me look at her, Grandfather. I don't want to feel what she's going through—

"Her name is Windflower, in the white man's tongue."

Turning towards the still little body. "Her spirit has fled."

"It has not. Help her find her happiness and you will find your own. Remember: Windflower."

"Windflower," Red Dove repeated. When she turned again to look at him, all she saw was a pile of rags on the floor.

"Grandfather!" she screamed.

"What's the matter, Red Dove?" Jerusha cried, rushing over.

"Grandfather... was here... I know he was." Red Dove was sobbing now, because she *did* know. He *had* been there—but in spirit, not in life.

She stared at a beam of light that found its way through the small high window above the altar and lit the dust motes dancing in the air. She watched it crawl slowly across the floor, until at last it came to rest on her shoulders. She felt the glow of warmth that rose from her chest and spread outward across the room.

"Grandfather," she whispered, as she rose on trembling legs and stumbled towards the little girl. She looked at the still, small face, saw the eyelids flicker, and caught the ghost of a smile.

"You are living still," she murmured. She wanted to reach inside her pocket for the pouch, but remembered her grandfather's words and placed her fingers on her own bare throat instead. "The power is inside me now," she said, "so I know what to do."

She reached into the *parfleche*, pulled out the doll her mother had made and wrapped the little girl's fingers around it. "This is for you," she whispered, "because you are meant to live. And I will make you a promise: I will help you find your happiness, and through yours... I will find my own."

>> A Weapon <<

"You're very good to her, my dear," said Jerusha, bending over both Red Dove and Windflower in the cold chapel, now empty of all but a few of the wounded. "This is the last of them, thank God. We should go home now, too." Her bright, birdlike eyes scanned the room. "Sometimes I wish *we* had a weapon. Something so powerful that the men who did this would *have* to understand. Something that would make them feel the pain they caused, show them the truth."

Something like the pouch? Maybe the best weapon *is* the truth.

Jerusha put her hand to her forehead. "Forgive me. I don't know what I'm saying anymore. I'm so exhausted that I'm not really making any sense." Her shoulders slumped.

You are, thought Red Dove, more than you know. "What would you do if you had something like that?"

"It would be wonderful, wouldn't it?" Jerusha answered with a faint smile. "We could use it to fight against all this." She swept the air with her hand. "If people had to live it for themselves... feel it—"

"They would know the suffering they caused," said Red Dove, finishing the sentence for her. "And understand."

"Yes." Jerusha's eyes bored into Red Dove. "And the killing would stop."

"So we should give it to them," Red Dove thought out loud—and then realized she had said too much.

"Give what?" Jerusha frowned.

"Nothing. I mean, maybe we should challenge the soldiers, make them face what they've done... show them."

"I see." Jerusha tilted her head. "Are you really that brave, my dear?"

I don't know, thought Red Dove, as she watched ideas taking shape in Jerusha's head.

Jerusha had a steely glint in her eye. "If we brought the soldiers here—the ones in charge, that is—they could see what they've done, all the harm they've caused, and they would be *forced* to understand. We should go to the fort—"

"I can't go there! I'd be a captive again."

"I wouldn't let that happen."

I doubt you could prevent it, Red Dove thought, remembering Jerusha's inability to protect her before. "Besides, I can't leave *her*," she blurted, nodding at Windflower.

"We've done as much as we can here; there's hardly anyone left to care for, and there are others, finally, to look after them." She nodded at an efficient-looking woman in a clean white apron. "So we should go where we can do more good." Jerusha hesitated. "But of course, you don't have to if you're afraid—"

"'Fraid of what?" asked Rick, sidling over.

"Of going back to the fort," said Jerusha.

"Why would you do that?" asked Rick with a puzzled frown. "Thought you was headed to *Paha Sapa*."

"I was." Red Dove looked at Rick, then Jerusha, and finally down at the figure of Windflower, lying on the ground.

The woman emerged from the kitchen, a linen towel in her hands. She walked over to Windflower, bent down and picked up the doll that had fallen from her tiny fingers. "Here, little one," she said with kindness in her eyes. "This belongs to you."

"It does," said Red Dove. "It was a gift I gave her, from my mother."

She stopped, looked at the woman as she tended Windflower, and back at the few survivors left in the room. Jerusha's right. Windflower deserves justice. They all do.

She reached up to touch her neck.

And I know how to get it.

"Let's go," she said, and headed to the door.

"What? Where?"

"To the fort, like you said."

"But... wait," Jerusha grabbed her shawl and bonnet and followed Red Dove out the door. "We'll take the buggy. It's a bit of a journey and it's getting dark—"

"I'll ride my pony," said Red Dove. Because I might need her if I have to get away.

"An' I'm comin' too," said Rick, scurrying up behind them. "Better get back so they don't think I'm a deserter."

>> You're Hers <<

The little party—Rick and Red Dove on horseback, Jerusha following in the buggy—rode steadily southward. Dusk fell as they finally approached the walls of the fort.

"State your business," shouted the sentry from the watchtower. "Say... that you, Rick? Where you been? We was worried about you."

"Bringin' back a runaway," Rick nodded at Red Dove. "From the school."

He means me, Red Dove thought with alarm. Will he turn me in?

She searched his face and his smile told her the answer.

"Chasin' after an Indian, huh?" the sentry chuckled and waved them in. "Cap'n'll be pleased to see you. Go on."

Jerusha snapped the reins and the wagon lurched forward. The ground inside the gate had been churned by boots and hooves into a slushy mass. Dim light shone through the dirty windows that surrounded the yard. Odors of coffee, tobacco smoke and manure filled the air.

Jerusha wrinkled her nose. "Where will I find the commanding officer?" she asked a soldier walking past.

"Colonel's away, but the captain's in there." He gestured towards a small, lighted window in the corner. "He's the one in charge til the colonel gets back."

Jerusha pulled the buggy to a stop, slid carefully down and tied the horses to the rail. "This way," she said to Rick and Red Dove as she stepped up onto the rough plank sidewalk and tapped on the door.

"Come in," barked a voice and Jerusha opened the door.

The overheated room smelled of liquor, sweat and damp wool. A brass clock ticked away on the mantelpiece over a smoky fire. A man in a dusty cavalry hat was slumped behind a desk in the corner. He leaned forward, put his elbows on the table and poured himself a drink from a small metal flask. "Whatcha want?"

Red Dove stared at his crooked right arm and steel gray eyes. I know him, she thought.

Then he sat up. "Rick? Where the devil you been?" His voice was thick with drink and colored with a strange foreign sound. He took off his hat. His head was covered with snow-white hair.

He's the one I saw when I was here with my mother.

"And what are you doing with these women, son?"

"I brought back a runaway, sir." Rick nodded at Red Dove.

"Runaway, eh?" the man chuckled.

"Yessir, from the school."

"Christ." The captain smiled and poured himself another drink. "All right then. I knew you weren't a deserter. I didn't raise you that way." He jerked a thumb at Red Dove. "So who is she? Come over here, young woman. You seem familiar. Have you been here before?"

"Yes." Red Dove took a deep breath. "With my mother... to trade."

"And who might you be?" he said to Jerusha.

"Jerusha Kincaide. And I'm here—*we're* here—," she looked at Red Dove, "to tell you something."

"What?"

"Your men have done a terrible thing... wicked... evil," Jerusha began, but her voice trembled so much it came out in faint bursts. "Someone has to speak up for the victims. Your men have killed innocents, women and children, people who meant no harm to anyone," Jerusha went on. She looked hopefully at Rick. "Tell him, Rick. You saw them, didn't you? At the church."

Rick didn't answer.

Jerusha looked back at the captain. "We simply want you to know what you've done. Come to the church and see the wounded—"

"I seen plenty of wounded in me day," said the captain. "And I don't need to see more. Now if you'll excuse me, I got work to do."

"But—" Jerusha tried.

"Sergeant, show these women out."

"Yessir." A burly soldier moved towards them. "This way."

Red Dove reached up for her pouch and then remembered it was in her *parfleche*. "Wait," she said, bringing it out. "Here." She extended her hand.

"A weapon?" In one swift movement, the captain crossed the floor and before she had time to act, he grabbed her fist and forced it open. His fingers closed around the pouch.

He's not supposed to touch it here, Red Dove thought.

"There's nothing there," he roared, and stared at his hand.

His eyes grew round, and he staggered back, pouch in his hand. "What's... happening?" He looked straight at Red Dove.

But he needs to be looking at the wounded, Red Dove thought, for it to work. He needs to feel what they've gone through. Maybe if he's looking at me and I'm thinking of them, he'll understand.

"Think of your mother," came a voice.

My mother?

Falling Bird.

"Falling Bird?" she whispered. And try as she might to focus on the victims, their wounds, their pain, her mind was filled with the image of her mother's gentle face.

The captain's mouth hung open as he gaped at her. "Falling Bird... ," he said, looking at Red Dove, but seeing someone else. Then he shook his hand, slowly at first, then frantically. "It's burning. God almighty, there's nothing there, but it's burning. An' I'm hearing things, seeing things... about you... and her."

"Who are you?" He pushed his face close to Red Dove, so close that she could smell the whisky on his breath.

The buzzing noise grew louder as she saw what he was seeing: memories of a beautiful black-haired woman in a deerskin dress. Her face was turned away, but from the toss of her head, Red Dove knew she was young and pretty and very much in love.

"You're hers, ain't you? Falling Bird's?" he repeated. "That means that you're my—"

"No," Red Dove ripped the pouch from his hand. She raced through the door, grabbed Wichinchala's reins and leapt upon her back.

"You're not my father—you can't be. You're a *soldier*," she shouted, galloping across the courtyard. "You're lying—and this thing is too," she cried, and hurled the little pouch into the muck.

>> Things That Are Lost <<

"*Paha Sapa*," said Red Dove, patting her pony. "That's where we're going. To find Mother. So she will say it's all a lie."

Red Dove looked at the snow-covered road ahead. The moon was waning, and in the dim light it was hard to tell which direction to go. Straight, she thought. North to *Paha Sapa*.

"Wait up!" she heard from behind.

Rick's bigger chestnut soon caught up with her little mare. He grabbed the reins and slowed both horses to a walk. "Why'd you hightail it outta there? Where ya headed?"

Red Dove didn't answer.

Rick reached his gloved hand in his pocket and pulled

something out.

The pouch.

"That's mine!" she said.

"Thought so. Found it lyin' in the mud... you must'a dropped it."

"I did... wait... can you see it?"

"Sure. Why not? Just a lump of leather. What's in it, anyway?" he asked, pulling off his glove, and picking at the leather with his bare fingers. "Not much, is it?"

"Don't touch it!"

But it was too late. Rick's fingers had connected with the pouch. The whites of his eyes grew round and words tumbled out. "Feel kinda strange... like... I can tell what you're thinkin'... an' feelin'. Huh." He shook his head. "Some kinda Indian magic?"

"Give it back."

He stared at Red Dove. "You just learned that the cap'n's your father, an' you ain't happy... ." He wrinkled his brow.

Red Dove looked straight ahead.

"I don't like the way it makes me feel," he said, squinting at her. "So here. It belongs to you."

"*Wopila*. Thanks," said Red Dove, taking it from him. "You must be a special person," she murmured.

"Why?" Rick asked with a grin.

Because you could see it when others couldn't, she thought, *and* it didn't hurt you. That means something... but what?

"Guess it tells you a lot about people, don't it?"

"*Han.*"

"So you can use it to see that the cap'n's really a good man—"

"He is?"

"Sure. Been a father to me. Adopted me a long time ago after he'd lost his own family. Found me wanderin' as a little kid. My parents were dead, killed by Indians they said."

The pale moon came out from behind a cloud and lit his face. "So can that thing do anythin' else?"

"Like what?"

"Help you find things?" His eyes sought hers. "My dog—"

"I know. It's missing."

"Yeah. Disappeared at the Indian camp the night before the battle. So can you use it to help me find him?"

"I don't know." Red Dove shoved the pouch back in her *parfleche*. "But I don't want to use it anymore. Especially not there. I'd have to feel the suffering of all the people who died."

"You're right," he said with a shrug. "It'd be too much." Then his eyes found hers again. "If you're tired, you can climb on up behind me. Give your pony a rest," he said with a shy smile.

Suddenly, all his thoughts—and feelings—came clear.

"I'm all right," she mumbled.

"Suit yourself," said Rick, pressing his lips together. "Didn't mean to offend you." He jerked his head up suddenly. "I thought you said you was headed to the Black Hills."

"I did. I was—"

"Well that ain't where we're goin'. Musta missed the fork back there, 'cause this here's the road to where the battle happened."

"It is?" Red Dove was startled that she could have made such a mistake. But she knew that if she did, it was for a reason.

"What's happening, Grandfather?" she whispered.

His voice came in answer, carried by the wind. "Do as I ask and honor them in the place they fell. At Wounded Knee."

>> Go Down and See <<

Snow softened the landscape as they rode, coloring the world a gentle blue-white.

"Black Hills that way," said Rick, nodding over his shoulder. "But there's another fork up ahead. You can take a left turn there."

"You'll let me go?"

"Sure. When I touched that thing," he nodded at the pouch, now buried deep in the *parfleche*, "I saw how upset you were, missin' your family an' all—"

His horse shied suddenly. "What's the matter, girl? Easy."

"Up ahead," Red Dove said, listening to the buzzing in her head. "I can feel it."

"What?"

"Chankpe Opi Wakpala. *Wounded Knee.*"

Rick brought his horse to a halt at the edge of the ridge, slid off, and tied her to a lifeless tree.

Terror gripped Red Dove as she approached, but she forced herself to look down at the valley below.

The sight that met her eyes was worse than she imagined. Bodies were there, unburied still, dozens and dozens shrouded with a layer of white and lit by the glow of the moon.

"Someone should put them to their rest," she whispered.

"What do you mean?" asked Rick, his eyes fixed on the devastation.

"Honor them. Lay them on *winchagnakapi*—scaffolds—and put them in the ground."

"They'll be sending a burial party from the fort soon."

"The *fort*? You mean the same men who *killed* them will *bury* them? That isn't right. We should do something first." She slid from her pony to the ground, walked to the edge of the cliff, and faced the death-covered valley below. She began to sing:

"Tunkashila Wakan Tanka ho nahoaho tuwa mis tate el kin,
Niya tuwa ku wiconi makaowacaga kilyuha kin,
Naho Aho mis. Mis cistila na hokesni.
Mis cin nita wasake na woksape."

"Never heard that before," said Rick, taking his hat off his head. "What's it mean?"

"This." Red Dove raised her arms and turned towards the valley again. "Oh, Great Spirit, whose voice I hear in the winds," she said, "And whose breath gives life to all the world, Hear Me. I am small and weak. I need your strength and wisdom." She looked at Rick, now kneeling beside her. "May *Wakan Tanka*, the Great Spirit, watch over you." Her voice lifted in the wind. "And may *your* spirits be at peace."

"Amen," sighed Rick, rising slowly and putting his hat back on his head.

Red Dove felt an icy finger down her spine. Something was calling her from below. "I have to go down. I have to see."

"Leave the pouch," a voice called. *"On the ground. There."*

Red Dove reached into the *parfleche*, pulled out the pouch and laid it on the frozen earth.

"Why'd you do that?" asked Rick, walking towards it.

"Don't touch it!" she warned and he moved back, watching as she stumbled down the icy slope to the valley below.

A tiny doll lay on the ground. But it wasn't a doll.

The rosebud mouth, soft round cheeks and snow-covered lashes were those of a child.

The blood froze inside her.

"You okay?" Rick called from the ridge. "Should I come too?"

His words were swallowed by a sudden roar, a blast of hooves from the ridge above.

"Stay down," he cried. "Hide!"

Hide? Huddled at the base of a cliff, Red Dove saw she was an easy target for a man with a gun. She slumped to the ground and forced herself still.

"Thought you'd beat me to it, huh, Rick?"

A chill went through her. Jake!

"What happened? You lose that girl you were chasin'?"

"No... I—"

"Lookin' for souvenirs, then? So am I. Indian stuff could be valuable. You find somethin' nice—it's mine."

Red Dove waited, stiff with fear, eyes squeezed shut, not wanting to see what was around.

Rick's voice broke through. "He's gone, Red Dove, lookin' for other stuff. Now's your chance."

Red Dove was shivering so hard no sound could emerge.

"Climb up. I'll help you."

She crawled to her feet on the slippery ground.

"Over there. Slope's gentler." Rick pointed to where the cliff wall met the valley floor.

There was a crunch of boots on icy ground. Red Dove fell back down.

"Who you talkin' to, Rick?"

"No one," said Rick with a nervous laugh. "Ghosts, I guess."

"Plenty of 'em round here. Ain't scared, are you?" Jake sneered.

"Nah. Course not. You find anythin'?"

"Junk. Nothin' valuable. Say, what was it I seen you pick up back at the fort?"

"What do you mean?"

"You know. Just outside the gate. I saw you stop your horse an' pick somethin' up off the ground that she dropped, most likely. What was it? Anythin' valuable?"

Rick shook his head. "Junk, like you said. Just a scrap of leather. I left it."

"You're lyin'." Jake squinted at Rick. "I can always tell. Give it here."

"Tell him to pick it up."

What? Red Dove, in her terror, squeezed her eyes shut again.

"Jake should pick it up. Tell him."

"He should pick it up, Rick," she whispered in words that only Rick could hear.

"Over there," Rick said. "See? That little bit of leather lyin' on the ground? Pick it up."

Red Dove opened her eyes and saw Jake's figure against the sky, moving to the edge of the cliff. He bent down.

"Ain't nothin' there."

He straightened, turned and looked down. "But I did see somethin' else. That girl down there. D'ya wanna see her twitch? Watch this." He pulled his gun from its holster, raised it, aimed and fired.

"No!" screamed Rick as the blast shattered the night and Red Dove's world went black.

>> Suspended Above <<

She felt herself rise. Gazing down, she felt an odd, lazy calm, knowing this struggle wasn't hers.

As if suspended above, she watched Rick. "Don't go," he whispered.

But I want to... .

A line of smiling ancestors, men in eagle feathers, painted for battle, women in bead-trimmed deerskin, waiting to take her home.

"Gray Eyes." Before her, the old, well-loved face.

I will stay with you now, Grandfather. Here. Forever.

She watched the light grow and swallow the dark, the line of dancers spiral into a new vision, a cloud of women dressed in purest white, nodding and smiling. "Follow us... ."

A song from far away, carried by the ancient wind, holding memories of everything her people ever knew.

"Do you want to leave the world?" her grandfather called.

I want to be with you. Wherever that is.

"I have taken the path to the Western Sky. I am no longer of the world you know—"

Then I will come too!

"Don't waste your time, kid." Jake's voice shattered the moment. "Burial party's comin' so let's get outta here."

Rick, frozen with shock or dread, didn't answer. He bolted down the slope to where Red Dove lay. "No!" he howled into the wind.

"Cryin' for an Indian? Get back here. Now."

Red Dove wanted to scream from above. Give him the pouch. It's lying there on the ground at the top of the cliff. Use it.

Rick looked up as if he'd heard. "The pouch," he said, and staggered back up the cliff to where the little bundle was lying.

"Whatcha got there, kid?" asked Jake, moving slowly towards him. "Give it here."

Rick ignored him. Wrapping the pouch in his bandana so as not to touch the leather, he picked it up, but instead of giving it to Jake, he went slipping and sliding back down the slope and carried it to where Red Dove was lying. "This has magic," he whispered and laid it on her chest. "It'll heal—"

"Whatcha got, I said?"

"Leave me alone, Jake!" Rick cried, head bowed as he watched for signs of life from Red Dove. She saw his shoulders heave, watched him brush his sleeve across his eyes and turn towards the man lumbering towards him. "You'll pay for this, Jake," he said, balling his fists.

"Yeah? Who's gonna make me?"

The pouch, Red Dove said again. The pouch!

Rick nodded as if he understood. "Here," he said, picking it up in his bandana and holding it out to Jake. "What she dropped at the fort. You said you wanted it. So take it—"

"You told me it was junk."

"I lied. It's worth a lot."

"Yeah? Then why're you givin' it to me?"

"Because… you should have it." Rick held out his hand.

Jake watched him suspiciously with his one good eye. "You tryin' to trick me? There ain't nothin' there—"

"You don't see it? Here. Catch." Rick took aim and hurled the pouch at Jake, who raised his arm to ward it off.

The pouch, like a living thing, leapt into Jake's outstretched palm. And stuck.

"What the—" Jake's fingers closed around the thing he couldn't see.

"Feel it?" Rick whispered. "In your hand?"

A shower of sparks rose from between Jake's curled fingers, and Red Dove knew what was coming next.

"It's burnin'," Jake cried, shaking his hand to be free, but his fingers wouldn't release. "Somethin's burnin'. Get it off!" He twisted and turned, leaning far over the edge of the cliff to fling it into the valley below, desperate to be rid of the pouch.

And saw the bodies.

"No… !" he cried, and as he did, Red Dove watched the memories of what had happened to the people lying there fill his head.

She saw him fix his eyes on a little girl lying near the base.

And become her,

Remembering,

She saw the soldiers of the Seventh Cavalry rush up, the bayonet slice down and down, through the sleeve of the robe and the flesh of the arm.

"Stop," Red Dove heard Jake cry, as pain roared through. She saw him, eyes drawn by some dark force across the field to a boy lying in a ditch,

Become him,

Remembering, reliving,

The race for safety, the bullets that shattered his chest.

"No," she heard Jake cry, trying to look away as his eyes were

dragged to a mother with a baby at her breast.

And watched him become her,

Reliving...

The infant's warmth,

The desperate panic,

The blow that stopped her heart... .

"It's me they're killin'! Because I am them, all of them!" Jake screamed.

Red Dove watched him fall, writhing in pain, lost in a nightmare that went on and on for what felt like forever, until, at last, he gave a great shuddering howl into the night.

"I'M SORRY... ."

The pouch fell from his hand.

"I didn't know," he whimpered, shivering on the ground. "I didn't know. I didn't know."

"What didn'tcha know, Jake?" said Rick, bending over to claim the pouch, careful not to touch the leather.

"What it was like, what I did."

"Yeah, well now you do. Because of this."

>> Gone <<

"Their tracks lead here, I think," called a man's voice, followed by the creak of a wagon.

Red Dove, still watching from above, listened to the sound of voices she knew.

"Over here, Captain," she heard Rick cry.

"That you, son? What the devil are you doing here? And who's that—Jake? Drunk again—"

"He shot her. Down there. She needs help!" Rick's words tumbled out in a rush. He pointed to the bottom of the cliff.

"Dear God!" Jerusha scrambled off the wagon.

The captain was quicker. He launched himself down the slope and fell to his knees next to Red Dove.

She saw him bending over her, fingers pressed to her wrist. "Come on, come on," he mumbled.

He's trying to save me.

"You gotta help her, Cap'n," said Rick, rushing up beside him.

"There's no need."

"What? I don't understand—"

"Let's just get her away from this terrible place," the captain choked.

Red Dove heard Jerusha's long wail, saw Rick rush down the slope to her side.

"Can't be," said Rick. "No." Rick shook her, gently at first, then harder as he refused to accept what the others knew.

"Stop, son," the captain said, laying a hand on Rick's shoulder. "She's gone."

From her vantage point above, Red Dove saw herself being lifted from the frozen ground, carried slowly up the long steep slope. And watched it all: the Captain holding her up; Rick, brushing his face with his sleeve; Jerusha sobbing.

Don't cry, she whispered.

Rick stopped and looked up.

"What is it, son?" asked the captain.

"Thought I heard somethin'. . . ," Rick pointed to the sky. "Up there."

"The wind. Come on, let's get going." The captain looked at Jake. "You did this," he said, darkness in his eyes.

>> Somethin's Changed <<

"What are we gonna do with Jake, sir?" Rick asked. "He shot her—"

"And for that he'll be punished."

"Will he?" Rick looked at the bodies around. "What about the others who did the killin' here? Will they be punished, too?"

"Good question," said the captain, scowling. "None of it makes a lick of sense now, does it?" He pulled a rope from the back of the wagon.

"Tie him on good and tight, Rick, so he doesn't fall off." The captain shook his head. "It would serve him right if he did."

"Remember anythin', Jake?" Rick whispered, as he wrapped the coils around Jake's slack torso. "Of when you were holdin' the pouch, I mean."

"The pouch?" Jake stared, bleary-eyed. "Was that what it was? That thing that you threw at me? Made me feel different somehow. Somethin's changed... I can feel it." Tears filled his red-rimmed eyes and rolled down his drooping mustache.

"Something's changed for you all right," said the captain, striding over. "Rick said you shot her. So if there's any trouble, soldier, any trouble at all—" He nodded at his holster. "Understand?"

"Yessir... there won't be no trouble, *sir!*"

"Good then." The captain climbed up on the wagon. "Ready?"

"Ready," answered Jerusha, huddled next to Red Dove. "Have you got a blanket... for her?" she asked.

"A blanket?" asked the captain, with a glimmer of hope in his eyes. "Is she—"

"No," said Jerusha. "I just thought… it's so cold."

"Yeah it is, so here," the captain said, taking off his coat and draping it carefully over Red Dove's still body. He climbed back onto the seat, jerked the reins and the wagon lurched forward over frozen ground, hooves and wheels crunching through icy snow, with Jake and Rick and Wichinchala, riderless, behind.

>> The Truth <<

Watching from above, Red Dove saw her motionless body lying in the back of the wagon. She listened to the sounds around her: the clatter of wheels, the pounding of horses' hooves, the voices. She heard Spirit's gentle panting, Jerusha's regular breathing as she dozed.

"There was so much I wanted to tell her," the captain said to Rick, riding slowly alongside "The truth. 'Bout me and Falling Bird."

Red Dove strained to listen.

"I'm her father, you know." The captain sighed. "I'd like tell you the rest, son, since you're bound to find out one day. I want you to hear it from me."

What's he telling him?

"You're almost sixteen, old enough. But for now this is just between us, understood? It's a hard thing for me to talk about—"

"You don't have to tell it, sir, if you don't want—"

"I do. I've wanted to get it off my chest for a long time. Maybe it'll help me understand why I did the things I did."

"Yessir."

"Well, it's like this… It was years ago and I was fresh off the boat from Ireland, excited about a new place, a new adventure. America. The West. When I saw Falling Bird, I thought she was the most beautiful thing I'd ever seen."

He's talking about my mother.

"Something just happened to me. Can you understand that?"

"If she was like Red Dove, well then, yeah, I can." Rick's voice trailed off.

Like me? A melting warmth ran through Red Dove. She waited for more, but there was silence.

The captain filled it. "Falling Bird was married before, to an Indian who got killed. She already had a son—"

"Walks Alone," Rick said.

"That's right." The captain shook his head. "I would've done anything for her—married her in the ways of her people, become one of them if I had to—just to be with her. They wouldn't allow it, me being a soldier and all. So she left them—her family, her home. Came to live with me. Got married in a church."

Mother never told me that.

"Did you live at the fort?"

"No. She stayed in a cabin nearby. And I sent Walks Alone away to school, so he'd learn our ways. She didn't like it, but I thought it was for the best. We were happy, mostly—until that trouble with Custer started. He was a fool. He just decided he could ride in to the Black Hills and take the gold, even though everyone knew that place was sacred to the Indians."

"So we went to war. I was called up, *had* to go, fight her people." The captain sighed. "It was my duty. D'ya see that, son? I had no choice."

"Course, sir."

"She didn't want me to, but I told her I'd be shot as

a deserter if I didn't. She gave me some kind of drink, a potion—Indian medicine, she said—to make me strong. But she lied. It made me weak. Next thing I knew, it was full daylight and the sun was shining in my eyes, blinding me. The battle had begun and she was gone." He paused. "It was at a place the Indians knew as the Greasy Grass, but our people just call it Custer's Last Stand. Because everyone died there, every last man." The captain stared into the distance. "Maybe they wouldn't have, if I'd been there."

"You really think you'd have made a difference?"

The captain shrugged. "Who knows? All I *do* know is I tried to climb up on my horse to join 'em, but was too weak from whatever it was she gave me. I fell off and broke my arm." He nodded at his crooked limb. "I staggered back to the fort with a good excuse, told them I'd been hurt too bad—"

"Which was true."

"Yeah, it was. Custer's defeat was so awful, no one spent much time worrying about a so-called deserter with a broken arm. The doc didn't even set it proper," he said bitterly. "Too busy getting ready to tend the wounded from the battle. But there weren't any. *All* our men were killed, every last one of them." His voice trailed off again.

"Ain't it better to be alive, sir? She saved your life."

"And took away my pride. I live with the dishonor to this day."

Rick went silent for a moment, then asked, "But what happened to her… Falling Bird, I mean?"

"I found out she was pregnant. With my child."

Rick lowered his voice. "Red Dove."

"Old Tom said the baby had gray eyes like mine, so she

looked different from them."

"Did you ever see her? The baby, I mean."

"No." The captain sighed again. "Falling Bird was still too angry."

"So what did you do?"

"Sent whatever I could, to help her through. I told Old Tom to leave supplies outside their tent at night so no one would know it was me sending them. But I got found out and had to stop." He paused. "And, well, by then, I had you to look after—"

"When you found me, after Indians killed my family—"

"You were the best thing that ever happened to me, you know? You made me proud. Still do. Every day."

"Thank you, sir," said Rick with a catch in his voice.

"So that's it, son," the captain went on. "The truth. Can you forgive me?"

"For what, sir? Like I said, you've been a good father to *me*. Sounds like *she's* the one you should have asked." Rick pointed to the back of the wagon.

"Yeah, and it's too late now . . ." mumbled the captain, pulling his hat brim down and hunching his shoulders against the cold.

Forgive him? wondered Red Dove, through the turmoil in her head. Can I?

"So now what're you gonna do, sir?"

"What *can* I do, after all the harm that's been done?" The captain went silent for a moment, then took a deep breath and continued. "Just wish she was still here so I could tell her all this myself."

"Yeah, sir," said Rick. "I wish she was too."

>> Decide <<

They look so sad, Grandfather, Red Dove called, *gazing upward.*

"They are sad. Very sad."

She saw his ageless eyes, his kindly face.

"They don't want you to go—"

But I want to be here with you, in this wonderful place. I don't want to be back in the world of the living—

"You are willing to leave the ones you see below?

Yes.

"And what of the others? Your brother and mother—"

My mother's alive? Where?

Grandfather didn't answer. Instead, her mother's face came into view, the smile warm and beckoning, and then it began to blur, as the figure receded and became that of a gray-haired old woman, hunched and rocking beside a dying fire.

What's happened, Mother? Don't be sad!

"How can she not be? She has lost her children."

Is my brother gone, too?

Another image came into view, that of a rough wooden scaffold with a knotted rope dangling from its center, and a tall, slender youth, dressed in buckskin, hands tied behind his back, climbing the steps.

Stop him!

"Who is there to do that, if you are not?"

Then another vision: a classroom full of dark-haired, dark-skinned girls, in high-collared dresses, covered with starched white pinafores. A tiny girl, shoulders slumped, chin in hand, fingers hiding an ugly scar coiled around her neck and chin. Looming above her a tall, black-robed figure, holding a stick.

Sister Agatha! Make her stop!

"How, if you are gone?"

Red Dove, stunned, didn't know how to answer. Tell me what to do, Grandfather, she said at last. I want to help—but I want to be happy, too—

"You will be, if you help them, down there."

But this is where there's happiness, Grandfather. With you—

"Happiness is everywhere, Gray Eyes."

No it isn't. Not down there.

"It is, if you look. Remember the promise you made to that girl?"

Which girl? Windflower?

"You said you would help her find her happiness. If you do that, you will find your own. You threw the pouch away, but it has returned. Will you accept its challenge? Decide."

His voice began to fade.

Grandfather?

No sound now, only silence; no light, only dark.

I don't want to.

She remembered the crystal glow, the music, the smiles that surrounded her in the world she wanted to join.

"Decide," she whispered through parched, blue lips.

And felt herself falling, dragged by the weight of stone on clay, down to the iron-hard coldness of the world she knew, the icy bones of earth.

≫ Honor Them ≪

A shout brought Red Dove to consciousness. She felt hardness of the wagon beneath her and cold air on her face.

"She's alive, Captain!" cried Jerusha from what seemed very far away. "Dear God, she's alive!"

Bludgeoned by a pain so intense she couldn't speak, Red Dove opened her eyes, but saw nothing. The miraculous light was gone, the peace and happiness she felt disappeared and something foul pricked her nostrils.

When her vision cleared, Jerusha's face was above her, hand over mouth to stifle a sob. "A miracle," she murmured.

The wagon stopped. Rick and the captain jumped off.

"A miracle," said the captain. "I never thought—" Through half-lidded eyes, Red Dove saw him wipe away tears as he gazed down at her.

Again, Red Dove tried to raise herself, but her arms shook and her head was dead weight on her useless body. The pain came and went, sometimes overwhelming, sometimes hardly felt—until another wave hit and she had to grit her teeth against it.

From where she lay, she could see bursts of lightning dance across the sky, turning the landscape behind them an eerie gray. She shut her eyes again.

"There," she heard her grandfather's voice as another shaft of light lit a spot where more bodies lay. She saw an old man, head wrapped in a white bandana, his arms reaching skyward in a frozen embrace.

Is it... you?

"No, you will not find me, so do not look. But honor him. And all those lying back there.

"Go back and honor him," she whispered.

"What? Don't try to talk, dear," said Jerusha. "Save your strength." Red Dove felt Jerusha's cool hand on her brow. "Let's get her out of here. And hurry."

"Right you are," said the captain, climbing back onto the wagon. "Time's wasting—"

Another flash of silver pierced the air, waking Red Dove.

"Wait," she croaked, pointing weakly. "Honor him first. Back there."

Rick seemed to understand. He turned to face the fallen warrior. "To you and everyone else who died here as well," he said, pulling off his hat and making the sign of the cross, "may *Wakan Tanka*, the Great Spirit, watch over you." His voice lifted in the wind. "And may your spirits be at peace."

May your spirit be at peace as well, Grandfather, Red Dove echoed in her thoughts.

"What the... hey, wait!" Rick cried, as a shape lurched out of the darkness and propelled itself at him with a force that knocked him flat. With one hand, he shielded his body; with the other, he tried to push the wild creature away.

And then he saw.

"Spirit!" he cried, wrapping his arms around his wriggling friend, as the scruffy animal licked his face and danced around them all, delirious with joy.

Channaphopa Wi
The Moon-of-Popping-Trees
Jerusha's Cabin—Late Winter, 1891

❯❯ Justice ❮❮

"You awake?" Rick stood at the door to the room where Red Dove lay. A week had passed, but her recovery had been surprisingly swift. Now she was healing and grateful to be back with people who cared.

She sat up in bed, pulled at the blanket to hide the bandage that covered her throat and chin and ran her fingers through her tangled hair.

"Must be feelin' better if you're tryin' to fix yourself up," Rick said, walking in with a grin. "It's kind of a miracle the way you came through this." He closed the door behind him and scanned the room. "D'ya mind if I sit down?" he asked, pointing at the chair beside her bed and dropping into it.

"Cap'n's gone back to the fort to see 'bout the court martial."
Rick's darkly tanned forehead was creased in a frown. "D'ya
know what that is?"

Red Dove shook her head. She could read his thoughts,
but that required effort and she was still too tired. It was easier
just to listen for the answer.

"Military justice. Might mean prison for the commandin'
officer—"

"My father?"

"No," soothed Rick. "Your father's only a captain. It's
Colonel Forsyth they're after. The general wants him charged
for gettin' people killed." Rick jerked his head towards the
window. "Back there at Wounded Knee."

"For killing my people?" Red Dove's heart leapt at the
thought of a white man's court finally bringing justice.

Rick shook his head. "No one's gonna get court martialed
for that. He'll be tried for gettin' his *own* men killed. Soldiers.
In the crossfire from their guns."

"That isn't real justice."

"Maybe not, but it's better'n nothin'." Rick shifted his hat
from one hand to another. His tawny face broke into a nervous
smile. "I have somethin'… that belongs to you."

It wasn't the pouch, Red Dove knew. That was tucked
safely back in her *parfleche*. She watched him reach into his
pocket, pull out a small beaded object and place it on the sheet
next to her.

"My amulet! The one my mother gave me." She stared at
the bits of blue and yellow glass, the familiar turtle shape.

"You dropped it at the fort that day. Had it the whole time,"
Rick said with a sheepish grin. "Just didn't know how to give it

to you, and the longer I waited, the harder it got." His eyes crept over her face. "Jake said it was worth somethin', that I should sell it, but I knew that was wrong. It *was* worth somethin'. But to you, not me." He shifted his gaze to the floor.

He had it all the time, she thought, and didn't know what to say.

"I'm sorry," he mumbled.

She touched the intricate beadwork and looked at his troubled face.

"I know you are," was all she could manage, forcing the words through her lips.

"Honest. Can you see your way to... forgive me?" Rick met her eyes for an instant, then slid his away. "Well, best be goin'." He rose, turned and headed for the door.

"Wait."

He stopped and jerked his head around.

Red Dove reached for the *parfleche* and pulled out the pouch. "You can see this, can't you?" she said, holding it up.

"Course. Why'd you ask?"

"Not everyone can. Only certain people." Red Dove watched his face, remembering his courage, appreciating his kindness as if for the first time.

"Strange," Rick said with a shrug. He shoved his hat back on his head and turned to leave.

Red Dove hesitated for a moment, then decided. "*Wanagi...* ," she said, "*washte.*"

Rick stopped in his tracks. "Naggy what?"

"*Wanagi* means Spirit. The name of your dog in my language. And *washte* means good. It would be good if you brought Spirit... when you come to see me, that is."

"Come to see you?" Rick's face lit up. "Yeah? Really? You know I'll come find you wherever you are." He nodded so hard his hat fell off. Laughing, he bent to pick it up. "*Wanagi... washte...* means Spirit... good. Guess I learned somethin' today, didn't I?"

Yes, thought Red Dove. You did. And so did I.

>> He Lives with the Spirits <<

"Finished with that plate yet? Jerusha'll be back any minute an' she'll wanna have this place cleaned up," said Old Tom to Red Dove, as they sat with Walks Alone at the little wooden table. "You're lookin' a whole lot better, you know? Bullet just grazed you. Don't hardly show."

Red Dove pulled the shawl up to cover her still-bandaged throat and chin. Jerusha had tried to hide the mirror, but Red Dove had read her thoughts, found it and taken a look. She didn't like what she saw.

"Won't look near so bad in a couple o' weeks," said Old Tom.

He's probably right, Red Dove thought, remembering Windflower's horrible wound and the scar she would carry for life.

"Say, what're *you* looking at?" Old Tom followed Walks Alone's gaze through the window that faced west. "Pretty, ain't they, the hills of the *Paha Sapa*? Guess that's why your people love 'em so much."

Walks Alone tilted his head. "That's where I'm going."

"Yeah? But what if the soldiers find you and force you back to the school?"

"Then I'll run away. And I will keep running away

until they finally leave me alone." Walks Alone squared his shoulders. "Why don't you come with me? And find out why we love them so much."

"Huh?" said Old Tom, wrinkling his forehead.

"You respect our people, our ways. You're a good man. Come with me to *Paha Sapa*."

A broad smile lit Old Tom's face. "You know, I'd kinda like that." Then his face clouded over. "But I can't leave Jerusha. Who'd look after her?"

"Come with us," said Walks Alone. "We'll live as we always have."

"I made a promise to stay and help," Red Dove said, thinking of Windflower.

Red Dove got up, walked into the bedroom and sat on the bed. Her eyes blurred, her chin throbbed and the bandage round her throat scratched and pulled at the slowly healing wound. She didn't want to think about the future— but had to. She listened to the murmurs coming from the kitchen. Then she heard the door open and close as Old Tom went out.

"Say what you mean, Sister," Walks Alone said, coming into the little room where she was sitting. "What promise did you make? And when?"

"I told Grandfather I would help that little girl, the one with the terrible wound at her throat."

"When?" asked Walks Alone with a puzzled frown.

Red Dove saw the confusion in his face. She knew she would have to explain but didn't want to. She got up and walked to the window to put off telling her brother that their grandfather was gone. Through the wavy glass, she saw Old

Tom place a piece of wood on the chopping block and raise his axe. "Jerusha wants me to stay here with her," she said, trying to change the subject.

"Is that what *you* want?" said her brother in a soft voice. "Tell me the truth. There's no one to hear us. Old Tom's outside and Jerusha's gone to town."

"It's better than going back to the school... or the reservation."

"Better than living like a prisoner, you mean," her brother said with scorn in his voice. "Come with me to *Paha Sapa*, where we belong—"

"*Is* it where we belong?" said Red Dove, shouting now, as surprised as her brother at the anger surging up inside her. "How long will that last? How long will *Paha Sapa* belong to us, do you think?"

"Forever. The hills are ours. We'll find our mother and grandfather there—"

"Grandfather—" Red Dove said with a catch in her throat.

Walks Alone stepped closer, an angry challenge in his eyes. "What?"

"He lives with the spirits now—"

"How do you know?"

Red Dove ducked her head, not wanting to see the hurt on her brother's face. "He was there. At Wounded Knee."

"You saw him?"

"In a vision. He said he went there to find you—"

"He died there because of me?" Walks Alone turned his back on his sister and clenched his fists.

"It wasn't your fault—"

"It was." He turned around and the look on his face frightened Red Dove. She put her hand on his arm but he shrugged it off.

"Don't do it," said Red Dove, seeing what was in his head, watching him swing his body up to climb a wall of rough-cut timbers, covered with nicks and gashes.

The fort!

She saw him lift an arrow from his quiver, fit it to his bowstring and aim at a white-haired soldier in the courtyard below.

"Don't do it," she said again. "Remember the ways of our people. We do not hate—"

"I *have* to," he said, heading for the door. Then he turned back suddenly. "There was someone else there—"

"At Wounded Knee? Who?" Red Dove asked, though she saw that as well.

"Your father. His hair was white, but his face was the same as when I was small. Probably he killed Grandfather."

"Stop, Brother!" Red Dove reached out to grab his sleeve, but he pulled from her grasp, stalked out of the room and slammed the door.

≫ Indians! ≪

A half-day's ride over miles of snowy road lay between Red Dove and the fort. She dug her heels into her pony's sturdy flanks and urged her on, hoping for a glimpse of Walks Alone, always a few lengths ahead.

"Who's there?" called the sentry, when the walls of the stockade finally loomed up, silhouetted against the late afternoon glare.

Walks Alone was nowhere in sight.

"I have to see the captain," Red Dove answered, looking nervously around for any sign of her brother. "It's urgent."

The sentry shifted position, blocking the sun that shone behind him, and for a moment Red Dove had a clear view of his face—and the round black patch that covered his eye.

Jake! Why isn't he in jail?

"He ain't seein' nobody today, 'specially not an Indian, so go back where you come from."

Red Dove swiveled Wichinchala out of the gate, but instead of turning back to the road, she rocketed around to the side of the fort. There, in front of her, were the rough-cut timbers she had seen in her dream, covered with nicks and gashes gouged deep into the walls of the stockade.

"Wait here," she whispered to her pony.

She slid off, looking for a way up. Digging her leather-covered toe into a gap, she reached for the lowest crevice, a foot above her head.

Give me strength, Grandfather, she prayed, as a surge of adrenaline coursed through her. Slowly, carefully, she pulled herself up the bark-covered wall. Up and up she climbed until, with her last ounce of strength, she flung her torso onto the narrow walkway at the top.

Crouching before her was Walks Alone, fitting an arrow to his bow.

Down in the courtyard was her father.

"Don't," she whispered.

Walks Alone swung around, the arrow pointing at her.

"Go away," he hissed and aimed it back at the captain.

"Grandfather wouldn't want this—"

"Grandfather isn't here!" Walks Alone narrowed his eyes and raised his bow.

"He *is* here, Walks Alone," pleaded Red Dove. "He's with us all the time. He wouldn't want this, please—"

Walks Alone pulled the bowstring tighter. "Leave me alone."

He let go.

The bow shuddered and the arrow arced high into the air.

But instead of piercing the breast of the man below, it rose even higher, and came to land in two neat pieces beside her brother's foot.

"What?" he murmured, eyes round with amazement. He nodded at the quiver lying next to Red Dove. "Give me another. Quick!"

"No," something whispered inside her.

Walks Alone, eyes fixed on the courtyard below, reached out his hand for the arrow, but Red Dove pulled back.

"No," she echoed.

"Summon the pouch," the voice whispered.

I can't! I left it… at the cabin. It's not here!

"Summon it and it will come."

Red Dove stared at her brother, his hand still outstretched, waiting for the arrow.

"I summon the pouch," she said in a small soft voice.

She felt a tingle, an itch, a burning sensation, and the small gray bundle appeared in her hand.

"This is what you need, Brother," she said and placed it gently in his palm.

"What?" He looked down at the bit of shriveled leather. "It's not a weapon—"

"It's better than a weapon."

An odd look appeared in Walks Alone's eyes as he stared at the little object. "An *opahte*," he murmured.

"You see it?" Red Dove asked.

"Yes. But I feel… odd," he gasped.

Red Dove watched her brother's face as the pouch began to work. *She saw what he saw, heard what he heard, felt what he felt, looking at the man below: the captain's loneliness, the constant ache from an arm that never healed, the shock of recognition when he saw Walks Alone crouching at the top of the stockade.*

She watched their eyes meet.

"It's you, son, isn't it?" the captain said. "Walks Alone? Thought you'd be coming for me one day. What's that you got there… a bow? Well, if you're gonna do it, do it now," he said evenly.

The bow shook. Walks Alone raised it high to steady it, held it for a moment, then lowered it to the ground. "I can't," he whispered, and dropped the pouch.

Red Dove picked it up.

"It's all right, son," said the captain, as if he could hear him. "Why don't you just come down now, and no one will get hurt—"

"Who you talkin' to, Cap'n?" yelled Jake. "An' what's that you're lookin' at… hey!" he shouted, seeing Walks Alone and Red Dove crouched on top of the stockade, with no easy way down.

Will he turn us in, Red Dove thought with alarm, or will he be different now, because of what he went through with the pouch?

She held her breath, waiting.

"Say, ain't you the one I seen? The one I shot? What was it you used on me back there? Some kinda witchcraft?" Jake lifted his rifle and aimed. "Indians!" he yelled.

Before she and Walks Alone could find an escape, Jake's shouts brought a swarm of soldiers out of the barracks, up onto the ladders and across the walkway.

Red Dove and Walks Alone were trapped.

"Hold your fire, men!" the captain called. "Let them come down. They didn't mean any harm—"

"Didn't mean no harm, huh?" called Jake. "That Indian was aimin' to kill you. An' that's a hangin' offense. Ain't that right, sir?" he asked a man who was just coming out of the officers' quarters.

"Yes," said the colonel, shading his eyes as he looked at Red Dove and Walks Alone. "So lock 'em up."

≫ A Hangin' Offense ≪

Darkness drifted through the tiny jailhouse window as Red Dove sat waiting on the rusty bunk of the narrow cell, her brother pacing beside her. The air in the room was thick, the silence interrupted by an occasional curse from one of the guards outside.

"What are they going to do to us?" whispered Red Dove.

"Hang us probably. Or me at least. You're innocent."

"But if I had given you an arrow, you would have been able to protect yourself—"

"*Hau.* I would have killed him."

"You would have," said Red Dove sadly.

"But I didn't," said Walks Alone, "because of that." He

nodded at the pouch lying on the bunk beside her. "Something happened when you gave it to me. I saw what he was. I felt I was him. And I couldn't—"

"I'm sorry, Brother. It made you weak—"

"It made me strong," said Walks Alone. "It gave me a kind of power."

"It's what Grandfather wanted." Red Dove didn't know what else to say. She listened to the silence in the room.

Walks Alone broke it. "They can't punish *you* for what happened, Sister. *You* tried to stop me.

From behind, they heard the creak of a key in the latch, as the captain, with Rick following, swung the door wide and burst into the cell. "Sentry's drunk and passed out, but there's no telling for how long." He grabbed Red Dove's arm, waved at Walks Alone to follow and hurried them through the darkened jailhouse and into the empty courtyard. "Horses are over there." He pointed at Wichinchala's shaggy shape and Walks Alone's sturdier mount.

He turned to Red Dove. "If you ever need anything, just get word to me through Old Tom." He wanted to say more, Red Dove knew, but shook his head instead. "Leave. Now."

"That man with the eye patch. Jake," blurted Red Dove. "You said he'd be punished for trying to kill me, but he wasn't. He was the guard—"

"Yeah," said the captain. "They decided he was only doing his job... I'm sorry, real sorry about the way things turned out—"

"If you're sorry, then there's something you can do."

"What's that?" the captain asked, heaving the heavy crossbar to open the gate.

"Make sure no soldier ever gets a medal for what they did at *Chankwe Opi*," Red Dove said.

"*Chankwe* what?"

"Wounded Knee," Rick answered for her.

"A medal? Hah!" The captain spat in the dirt. "No one will ever get a medal for *that*," he said, as he slapped the pony's rump, and together, Red Dove and Walks Alone galloped away.

›› *Toksa* ‹‹

At a steady gallop, hearts pounding to the rhythm of horses' hooves, Red Dove and her brother put miles between themselves and the fort. They had been riding steadily north half the night, and now it was close to morning.

"We're safe now," Walks Alone said, looking back. "There's no one following." He slowed his pony to a walk.

"Do you still hate him, Brother, even after what he did for us?" Red Dove asked.

"Who, the captain?" Resting both hands on the animal's neck, Walks Alone stared at the trail behind them. Then he turned to face his sister. "I didn't tell you before. When I was holding the pouch, I heard something... a voice."

"Grandfather? What did he say?"

"What you told me: we do not hate."

Red Dove tried to read her brother's face through the morning darkness. She saw the doubt in his mind. "It is not our way," she said softly.

"What about you, Sister? Can *you* forgive him?

"I already have." She pulled her blanket tight around her shoulders.

"So what will you do now?" her brother asked. "Come with me to *Paha Sapa*?"

Red Dove answered with another question. "Do you remember that girl, Windflower? The one with the terrible wound in her throat? I promised Grandfather I would help her... if she's alive, that is."

"She is alive. Old Tom told me. They're sending her to the school—"

"She won't survive there." Alarm rose in Red Dove. "Now I *know* what I have to do."

"What's that?" Walks Alone stopped his horse abruptly. Even in the dim light she could see the concern in his eyes.

"Go back to the school and get her out—or she won't last long there."

"And neither will you, Sister. Don't do it."

"I made a promise I have to keep." Red Dove heard the words coming out of her mouth. "Will you wait for me in the hills?"

"Yes, but I don't want you to go. I might never see you again."

"I have to. I'll come and find you. Later."

Walks Alone turned away, anger in his face. "You might not make it... but you're so stubborn. You always have been. Once you've made up your mind, nothing will change it, will it?" He shook his head. "All right then, go." His voice softened. "Should I come with you?"

"No, Brother, it's too dangerous. The soldiers will be looking for you."

"They'll be looking for you, too."

"I wasn't holding the bow when we were caught. I'll take

my chances." Red Dove shrugged. "I'll only be there long enough to get Windflower and then we'll both come find you in *Paha Sapa*."

"Do what you must, Sister. If that's the path you've chosen, then we will part soon." In the glow of the setting moon, Red Dove could see his sorrow. "That fork up ahead? That's where the road will split."

"Yes," whispered Red Dove, swallowing tears.

"You're sure? You're not coming with me now to find... Mother?"

"I promised Grandfather—"

"Grandfather," said Walks Alone sadly. Through the shadows he searched his sister's face. "Then this is where we say goodbye."

They rode in silence as a cloud crossed the moon. In the darkness Red Dove couldn't see his tears. But she knew they were there.

When they came to the fork, she reached out to touch his hand and, palm to palm, they said goodbye.

"*Toksa*, my brother."

"*Toksa*, my sister.... We will meet again."

>> Iyeska <<

The school loomed before Red Dove in the gray dawn light. Weary from riding, she stared at the vacant windows, the walls of stubborn brick, the silent bell tower.

This was where she needed to be, this place she had first seen in the Moon-of-Falling Leaves when nights gave only a hint of frost. But that was behind her now, and soon the earth would be warming.

By then I'll be safe in *Paha Sapa* with my brother and mother and Windflower.

Wichinchala whinnied in protest. "Shhh," Red Dove whispered. "There's nothing to fear."

Though Red Dove herself was afraid. No one knows I've come, she thought. I could still change my mind and go. Instead, she slipped off Wichinchala, tied her to a rail and walked up to the entrance. Twisting the iron knob, she pushed and the heavy door gave with a groan. Barely breathing, she stepped into a place that haunted her dreams. It was the same dank corridor, but different somehow: smaller, colder than she remembered—and empty.

Give me strength, Grandfather!

Footsteps clattered in the distance and Sister Agatha's ghostlike face came into view. "You've returned," said the nun with menace in her voice. "Wise choice. I knew you wouldn't last long out there."

"I'm... just here to find Windflower," Red Dove said, keeping her voice as steady as she could, although her knees were shaking.

"No idea who that is. And look at you," Sister Agatha snickered, pointing at Red Dove's deerskin dress and leggings, the *parfleche* bag slung across her shoulder. "Still dressed like a heathen." She grabbed Red Dove's arm with her bony hand and shoved her towards the stairs. "Get out of those filthy rags now. And then come and see me."

Red Dove clung to the banister. Her senses reeled and her legs wobbled, but she managed to climb. When she reached the landing, she looked down at Sister Agatha's black-robed figure, striding away.

Help me, Grandfather. Tell me where to find Windflower, so I can get her out of here.

She waited, and at last heard the familiar, thrumming drone, faster now and more intense.

"Look in the room where you used to sleep," the voice said.

Red Dove hurried to the dormitory as fast as her legs would go. She's not here, Red Dove thought sadly, looking at the empty metal beds. She must be with the others downstairs. She reached into the *parfleche* and pulled out the pouch.

The light in the room began to change. A shaft of iridescent blue refracted through the tiny glass window and pierced the morning shadows below the metal bed that once was hers.

"There," her grandfather's voice said.

Red Dove knelt down and pulled at the loose floorboards and a small, rose-tinted feather wafted into the air.

The one my mother gave me that day at the fort. I didn't know I left it.

She plucked it from the air and put it back in her *parfleche* next to the pouch. Pushing aside the splintered wood, she explored the gap with her fingers. Below it was another small crevice.

Why didn't I see this before?

She felt something.

A letter?

She pulled it out, brushed off the dust and began to read:

December 16, 1890

My Dearest Red Dove,

Sister Agatha sent me away because I knew too much. Now I must warn you about the danger you are in.

I told you that long ago, back in Ireland, she was in love with a soldier who abandoned her and the child she was carrying, and that after she lost that child she came to this country, looking for revenge. What she found when she got here filled her with even more rage and hate: he had married an Indian woman and had a child by her.

That man was your father, and that child, you.

So be careful! Get away if you can. And use the gift I leave you now: my cross. You didn't accept it before because it didn't work for you, but try once more. It may help you find what you need.

You are on a journey, my brave little friend. You told me a word from your language once—Iyeska? You said it meant someone who traveled between worlds, who explained those worlds to others, and who brought them together.

Be that person now: Iyeska.

And one day, if God is willing, come and find me so we can be together once again.

In God's love always,
Sister Mary Rose

Hands trembling, Red Dove folded the note and pushed the fragile pages into her *parfleche*.

I *will* find you, Sister. I promise.

She reached to the bottom of the crevice and felt what she knew had been lying there all along: the Celtic cross.

She held it up and waited. Slowly the metal began to warm to her touch.

"Grandfather?" she whispered.

"Find Sister Agatha," his voice answered.

But I have to find Windflower and get her out of here.

"First find Sister Agatha," his voice insisted, "and you will find what you need."

>> Summon the Pouch <<

Red Dove's hand shook so much her knock was too faint to be heard. She tried again.

"Enter," called Sister Agatha.

The nun sat in her high-backed chair, her long gnarled fingers toying with a leather belt. "I told you to change your clothes," she said, narrowing her eyes at the strap.

Red Dove's legs began to give way. "I just came to find—"

"Do you think you have a choice—what now?" Sister Agatha snarled, as a knock interrupted them.

The door creaked open and Sister Gertrude barged in. "Here is anuzzer vun," she said, thrusting Windflower into the room.

Sister Agatha recoiled at the sight of the vivid purple scar that snaked across Windflower's throat and chin. "She's hideous."

Red Dove rushed over and threw her arms around the cowering little girl.

"Her people dead. No vun know vat to do. Zey bring her here," said Sister Gertrude.

"Deal with her, then," said Sister Agatha with a wave. "I'm too busy. And I don't want to look at her any longer than I have to."

"You gif her name? Vat you call her?"

"Her name is Windflower," Red Dove tried.

Sister Agatha ignored her. "Let's see," she sighed, picking up the Bible and leafing through. "Where did we leave off? The last letter was 'm,' so 'n.'" She jabbed the page with her thumb. "Naomi. Means sweetness. She'll need all the sweetness she can get with *that* face." She stopped abruptly and turned to the little girl. "Naomi, are you listening? You have a new name."

Windflower stared up with terrified eyes.

"I asked you a question. Answer me."

"*Hiya*," Windflower whimpered, shaking her head in confusion.

"What?"

"*Hiya*. Means no in our language," said Red Dove. "She's telling you she doesn't understand—"

"Your language? She's forbidden to use it! And so are you." Sister Agatha looked at the belt.

Windflower, shaking like a small animal, darted for the door. But Sister Gertrude was quicker. She grabbed her, picked her up, and dropped her in front of Sister Agatha.

"Don't!" cried Red Dove, throwing herself between them.

Sister Agatha raised the strap.

Red Dove folded her arms around Windflower, as the first blow fell.

More beat down, covering Red Dove's neck, arms and legs with welts as she shielded the little body with her own. Through a blur of pain, she heard Sister Gertrude's mumblings, Windflower's whimpers, and Sister Agatha's labored grunts.

Grandfather, help! she begged, as the room spun around her.

"*Summon the pouch.*"

Red Dove could barely utter a word without releasing the screams inside her, but she gritted her teeth. "I… summon the pouch," she managed in a choked whisper. Then, in spite of the blows, she stood up, straight and tall.

Everything stopped. The room went quiet.

The nun, belt in hand, stood frozen in place. "What did you say?"

"I summon the pouch."

The sound of swarming bees filled the air.

"What pouch? What's happening?" Sister Agatha mouthed.

Red Dove watched the pouch, unseen by the nuns, emerge from the depths of the parfleche and begin to rise.

"What is it you're staring at?" whispered Sister Agatha, eyes round as she watched Red Dove follow the pouch's progress. She dropped the strap and stared upward, confused.

The pouch hung above her head, visible to Red Dove.

"What's there?" Sister Agatha raised her arms to ward it off. "Something I can't see?"

In answer, the pouch shot to her open palm. And stuck.

Sister Agatha went silent, gaping at what she now felt in her hand. Then she looked down, sensing something as a cloud of silver blue swirled from below her feet and spiraled up.

"No," she wailed, raising her arms against the blows she began to feel. "Why?" she screamed in horror.

"Why?" repeated Red Dove. "You know why!"

Windflower, wide-eyed with terror, started to tremble.

"It's all right," Red Dove soothed. "She's seeing what you saw, and hearing and feeling what she just did to us, because we're remembering it. It's the pouch at work."

"Ohhh," Sister Agatha moaned, lost in the agony she created.

Sister Gertrude crossed herself and backed towards the door. "*Teufel.* Devil!" she cried and ran from the room as fast as her swollen legs would go.

Panting and howling, Sister Agatha tried to shake herself free, but her fingers only closed tighter. "Get it off!"

She shook her arm… but the pouch held fast.

"Help me, someone help!" Sister Agatha roared.

"Tell her to look at you, now. And think of all she's done—the cruelty, the pain she inflicted when you were at the school. Send your thoughts back at her. Make her endure what you had to—and it will happen to her."

"Look at me," Red Dove said, spitting out the words and forcing herself to remember every blow, every beating, all the shame and betrayal.

I want her to suffer, Grandfather. She deserves it.

"She does, Gray Eyes, because she deserves to understand. But you must understand as well—"

Suddenly, Red Dove was no longer standing on the hard-polished floor of a cold, sterile school. Now she was in a smoke-filled cottage, surrounded by damp stone walls and a packed mud floor, watching a ragged man with rage in his eyes pull off his belt and raise it above a cringing little girl, landing blows on her neck, her arms, her shoulders.

Who's that?

"Sister Agatha—Maura then—when she was young."

I don't want to watch.

"You wanted to see her punished."

Not like this. She's too young. What did she do to deserve it?

"*Nothing. This is how she became what she is. This is how she learned to hate.*"

Red Dove felt something give way inside her. Her rage dissolved, replaced by a new emotion.

I feel… sorry for her, Grandfather.

"*You are feeling compassion, the remedy for hate—*"

So can we make the punishment stop?

"*She is the only one who can do that.*"

How… ?

As if in answer, Sister Agatha collapsed and fell into the chair. "I'm sorry," she whispered, uttering the words that would break the spell. "Truly, deeply sorry. Can you forgive me?"

The pouch fell from her hand.

Red Dove darted to pick it up. "Forgive you?" she shouted as she pushed it into the *parfleche* and started backing away. "How?"

"I'm sorry," the nun said weakly, "because I *do* know what it's like… to suffer." Her once glittering eyes were dull and glazed. "And I see… what you've been through—what I put you through."

Sister Agatha nodded weakly at Windflower, who was still shaking with fear. "What I did, what we all did. You *must* believe me. I understood your suffering when I remembered my own." She looked helplessly at Red Dove. A strange, wounded expression came into her face, one Red Dove had never seen before. "I don't want to cause any more pain. Please. I need you to… forgive me."

Red Dove glared back at her. "How can anyone forgive you after what you've done?"

"Try," said the nun helplessly. "I'll be different from now on—"

"*You'll* never change," said Red Dove.

"I will. After whatever… spell you put me under, I want to make amends."

"How?"

"I *am* a different person," Sister Agatha said, as if reading Red Dove's thoughts. "I *felt* the pain I caused you. From now on I am going to be kind. To her," she nodded at Windflower, "and to the others—but especially to you… even though I know you're his," she said softly. "Maybe because you *are* his."

His? Who… my father?

"You even look a bit like him. Those same gray eyes, that serious expression—"

"I can't believe you," said Red Dove, pulling Windflower towards the door, "after all you've done!"

›› Tell Him Where I Am ‹‹

"She hurt you, didn't she? Let me get some light so I can see." Jerusha touched a match to the wick and the lamp sputtered to life, erasing the shadows in her small, plain cabin. Then she reached across the rough wooden table to trace the mark, still vivid, on Red Dove's arm. "It must have been horrible."

"I'm all right," Red Dove shrugged, although the welts still burned. She looked around the neatly kept parlor. "If we could just stay here for a short while—"

"Of course." Jerusha adjusted the flame and the lamp spread its golden light throughout the room. "And you know I'll give you any supplies you need, but wouldn't it be better if you remained here a little longer before you went searching for your brother and mother? You could wait until spring, when it's warmer." She looked at Windflower. "She's been through so much. Don't you think she'd be better off here, where I can look after her?"

"It's safer in *Paha Sapa*," Red Dove answered. "The soldiers might come for me here."

"But didn't Rick say the captain got you a pardon?"

"Yes, but some soldiers—like Jake—might not honor it. In *Paha Sapa*, we'll be with our people. We'll all be better off." All except you, Red Dove thought, looking at Jerusha's weary face.

"I suppose you're right," Jerusha sighed. "At any rate, I'm glad you and Windflower came to me first. You know that if you need anything, I'll help. Thomas can always get word to me here—where I'll be. He wants to go live in the Black Hills with your brother—"

"I told you I wasn't going to, Sis. Can't leave you here."

"You should come with us," she said, though she knew Jerusha would never agree.

"No," Jerusha tapped her chin with her finger and turned to look out the window. "I can't live like you do, outside, in the wild. I have another idea. Sister Agatha asked you to go back and teach, didn't she? Why do you suppose she did that?"

"She needs teachers. A lot of the nuns have gone—"

"Yes, but she was different suddenly—kinder to you, you said. What made her change?"

"I don't know." Should I tell her about the pouch? Red Dove wondered. Grandfather said not to—and she wouldn't believe me anyway. "I won't go back, but maybe you should," Red Dove said to change the subject—and seeing what Jerusha was thinking.

"My thoughts exactly," Jerusha laughed. "You are such a little mind reader. Well, why not? I *was* a teacher once, back East—a good one. Wasn't I, Thomas?" She looked at her brother, who was bent over the toe of his boot. "Thomas? Are you listening?"

"What? Hole needs mendin'," he grumbled.

"I asked you a question. I was a good teacher, wasn't I? Maybe I should be one again."

"Sure, Sis." He looked up with a crooked grin. "Maybe you should. An' then I could go live in the hills."

"You could, Thomas, if it's what you really want." Jerusha then questioned Red Dove. "But can we trust Sister Agatha?"

Can we? wondered Red Dove. She remembered how the pouch had made Jake change for a while—until he took up his old ways again. Maybe the pouch can make people change—but only if they want to.

"It's a risk, I'll grant you," Jerusha went on, not waiting for an answer. "But one I think I might be willing to take. If things don't work out, I can always just leave. And the truth is… I've come to love you children." She nodded at Windflower, whose tousled head rested between her two arms on the table.

Jerusha took off her glasses, rubbed her tired eyes and peered at Red Dove. "*You* wouldn't consider it, would you, my dear?" she said, with a note of hope in her voice. "Come with me to teach."

"No," answered Red Dove. "If I did and things *didn't* work out for me there, I couldn't just leave. I'd be stuck." She nodded at Windflower. "And I made a promise to Grandfather. To help *her*."

"Ah, your promise. I know how much that means to you." Jerusha shoved her glasses back on. "You're so resourceful, I'm sure you'll find a way... out there. By the way—what if that young man, Rick, comes looking for you?" she asked with a sudden frown.

"Then tell him where I am," said Red Dove, ducking her head to hide the hopeful look she knew was in her eyes.

>> The Power is Inside Us Now <<

Red Dove sat in the moonlit room and looked around at the bark-covered walls, the cup of chamomile tea that sat cooling by the bed, her meager belongings.

She got up quietly, careful not to wake Windflower who was sleeping next to her, and crept to the window. Her cheek made contact with the icy glass and she stared through the lavender darkness at the vast prairie that led to *Paha Sapa*.

Wichinchala's tracks were still visible in the snow, a reminder of how far she had come that day.

She thought of the nuns remaining at the school. They would be crossing the yard on their way to evening prayers, before their nighttime rest. She thought of the cold, dark dormitory, the endless rows of hard metal beds, the lonely little graves on the hill—and the lifeless children lying there.

I won't let that happen to *her*, she vowed, looking at Windflower. Jerusha wants us to go back because she thinks things will be different now—but has Sister Agatha really changed? *Can* I trust her? And for how long? Soon it will be the Moon-When-the-Geese-Return, followed by the Moon-When-Leaves-Are-Green, and on and on through the seasons. Will she still be a kinder person then—or will she turn back into the monster she was before?

Red Dove strained to listen for an answer, but none came. She reached inside the pocket of her nightgown, searching for the comfort of the pouch.

Her fingers came up empty.

She felt in her other pocket.

Panic thrummed in her veins.

She picked up the *parfleche* and pulled it open.

There was the Celtic cross, lying next to the two feathers—one long and sturdy, from her brother, the other, soft and delicate, from her mother.

But the pouch had disappeared.

"Grandfather?" she whispered. Her heart was pounding, her blood pulsing in her ears. "Grandfather?" she tried again and listened long and hard, until at last, from the deepest, quietest place inside, she heard his voice.

"It has returned to the ancestors, where it belongs, Gray Eyes.

Why? I still need it!

"You do not... the power is inside you now. But if and when you do, then summon it and it will come—"

Will it?

"Yes. But use it wisely—along with the many other gifts that you possess—"

What other gifts?

"The gift of language, for one, of words."

What good are words, Grandfather?

"Words carry medicine, Gray Eyes; medicine that heals; medicine you share when you tell the story—and when you listen. With them you can travel between worlds and bring those worlds together. Remember, if you listen... you will be Iyeska.*"*

Red Dove was silent for a moment before another question pierced her thoughts. *What about you, Grandfather? Will you still be with me if I travel between worlds?*

"*I will always be there, Gray Eyes. Although you may not know it... so listen.*"

The voice began to fade.

I am listening, Grandfather. You talked about other gifts. What other gifts? What else? Red Dove asked.

But all she heard was Windflower mumbling in her sleep. She turned to look at the little face, the soft round cheeks, the jagged scar.

"*Listen,*" her grandfather's voice said.

She heard another sound then, from deep inside the parfleche, *like the music of crystal beads.*

She reached in and felt for the cross, then pulled it out and gazed at the intricate silver, the green and amber beads.

"*Will I travel between worlds to find you, Sister?*" she whispered, thinking of the nun whose friendship she so missed.

"*Courage is the other gift,*" her grandfather's voice said. "*The courage to listen, the courage to speak, the courage to choose—*"

I have chosen! I'm going to Paha Sapa *to find my mother and brother.*

Something wafted in the air.

The feather my mother gave me. Wasn't it in the parfleche?

She reached up, closed her fingers around it, careful not to crush its delicate fibers. She pictured her mother's well-loved face. I'm coming to find you, Mother, no matter what anyone says.

As if in answer, a shaft of moon glow lit the room and tinted it a rosy gray.

And you, Brother. She reached into the parfleche *and pulled* out the feather her brother had given her—and for a moment caught a glimpse of his face, hovering in the air beside her, wearing a smile before it disappeared.

"The courage to choose."

Then, suddenly, an odd, familiar smell pricked Red Dove's nostrils, that of musty wood, chalk dust and soap.

She closed her eyes and saw herself standing in front of a room full of dark-skinned girls, chanting a lesson. The light in the room was golden. The smiles on the faces were bright. Everyone was happy.

A little girl, sitting in front, raised her hand high, no longer afraid to show the vivid scar that coiled around her neck and throat.

"Maybe that is where I belong," murmured Red Dove, thinking of all the girls like Windflower that she had known and might come to know. "I made a promise to Grandfather that I would help find her happiness, and he said that if I did, I would find my own. But where is that—there, at the school? And how will I find the courage to face the soldiers… and Sister Agatha?"

"Listen."

And Red Dove did. She heard a sound from outside the window, a five-note trill.

A dove, my namesake.

She walked over to sleeping Windflower, dropped down beside her and touched her hand. "The courage to listen, the courage to speak, the courage to choose, Grandfather said. Because the power is inside us now… you see that, too; don't you?" Red Dove whispered as the tiny fingers closed around her own. "We *have* to go back. So we can help the ones who need us. And find the place where we belong."

Lakota Word List

Chankwe Opi—Wounded Knee

Han—Yes (for a woman to say)

Hau—Yes (for a man to say)

Hiya—No

Hoka—Let's go

Hoka Hey—Let's go (war cry)

Inahnio—Hurry

Iyeska—Person of mixed race, traveler between worlds, interpreter

Opahte—Pouch

Papa—Dried venison

Paha Sapa—Black Hills

Parfleche—Bag (from the French)

Pilamaya—Thank you

Toksa—We will meet again

Takoja—Grandchild

Tankashila—Grandfather, Great Spirit

Timpsila—Prairie turnips

Wakan Tanka—Great Spirit

Wakiyela Sha—Red Dove

Wana—Now

Wanagi—Spirit, shadow or ghost

Wanagi Wachi—Ghost Dance

Wanji, numpa, yamni—One, two, three

Wasichu—White people

Wasna—Dried meat and fruit patties

Washte—Good

Wicasa Wakan—Medicine man

Wichinchala—Girl

Wopila—We give thanks

Phrases:

Hehanni washte
Good day

Anpeta wakan washte
The day is holy and good (answer to the above)

The Seasons:

Kantasa Wi
The Moon-of-Ripe-Plums (August/September)

Chanwape Kasna Wi
The Moon-of-Falling-Leaves (October/November)

Heyunka Wi
The Frost Moon (November/December)

Wanichokan Wi
The Winter Moon (December/January)

Channaphopa Wi
The Moon-of-Popping-Trees (January/February)